THE ARMIES

EVELIO ROSERO is the author of seven novels and two collections of short stories, as well as several books for children and young adults. In Colombia his work has been recognized by the National Literature Award. *The Armies* won the 2006 Tusquets International Novel Prize in Guadalajara, Mexico, and the 2009 Independent Foreign Fiction Prize in the UK.

ANNE MCLEAN has translated books by authors including Julio Cortázar, Tomás Eloy Martínez and Juan Gabriel Vásquez. Her translations of novels by Javier Cercas have been short-listed for the 2008 Impac prize and awarded the 2004 Independent Foreign Fiction Prize and the Premio Valle Inclán.

"This finely-wrought but softly-spoken novel of love, war and grief not only laments a people's tragedy but celebrates the fragile virtues of everyday life at the end of its tether."
BOYD TONKIN, *Independent*

"*The Armies* is a disturbing allegory of life during wartime, in which little appears to happen while at the same time entire lives and worlds collapse . . . this is an important and powerful book." JANINE DI GIOVANNI, *The Times*

"*The Armies* is written in a compressed, lean style, which addresses the difficulty of the material with uncompromising clarity. It is a fragile tone, but Anne McLean's translation does full justice to it."
...my Supplement

Evelio Rosero

THE ARMIES

Translated from the Spanish by
Anne McLean

MACLEHOSE PRESS
QUERCUS·LONDON

First published in Great Britain in 2008 by MacLehose Press
This paperback edition first published in 2010 by

MacLehose Press
an imprint of Quercus
21 Bloomsbury Square
London
WC1A 2NS

Copyright © Evelio Rosero 2007

First Published in the Spanish language by
Tusquets Editores, Barcelona

English Translation Copyright © 2008 by Anne McLean

This book has been selected to receive financial
assistance from English PEN's Writers in Translation
programme supported by Bloomberg

A CIP catalogue reference for this book is available
from the British Library

ISBN 978 1 906694 77 7

10 9 8 7 6 5 4 3 2 1

Designed and typeset by Libanus Press, Marlborough
Printed and bound in Great Britain by Clays Ltd, St Ives plc

For Sandra Páez

N'y a-t-il point quelque danger à contrefaire le mort?
Molière

And this is how it was: at the Brazilian's house the macaws laughed all the time; I heard them from the top of my garden wall, when I was up the ladder, picking my oranges, tossing them into the big palm-leaf basket; now and again I sensed the three cats behind me watching from high up in the almond trees. What were they telling me? Nothing, there was no understanding them. Further back, my wife fed the fish in the pond: this is how we grew old, she and I, the fish and the cats, but my wife and the fish, what were they telling me? Nothing, there was no understanding them.

The sun was beginning.

The Brazilian's wife, the slender Geraldina, sought out the heat on her terrace, completely naked, lying face down on the red floral quilt. At her side, in the refreshing shade of a ceiba tree, the Brazilian's enormous

I

hands roved astutely along his guitar, and his voice rose, placid and persistent, between the sweet laughter of the macaws; this is how the hours proceeded on their terrace, amid sunlight and music.

In the kitchen, the lovely little cook – they called her Gracielita – washed the dishes standing on a yellow stool. I could see her through the unglazed kitchen window giving on to the garden. She swayed her backside, oblivious, as she worked: behind the short, very white skirt every bit of her body jiggled, to the frenzied and painstaking rhythm of her task: plates and cups blazed in her copper-coloured hands: occasionally a serrated knife appeared, shiny and happy, but somewhat bloodstained. I suffered too, apart from her suffering, from that bloodstained knife. The Brazilian's son, Eusebito, watched her on the sly, and I studied him studying her, he ducked under a table loaded with pineapples, she buried in the deepest ignorance, self-possessed, unknowing. He, trembling and pale – discovering his first mysteries – was fascinated and tormented by the tender white panties, slipping up through generous cheeks; I could not manage a glimpse of them from where I was, but, more than that: I imagined them. She was the same age as him, twelve. She was almost plump and yet willowy, with rosy glints on her tanned face, her curly hair black, like her eyes: on her chest two small hard fruits rose up as if in search of more sun. Orphaned early – her parents had died when our town was last attacked by whichever army it was, whether the paramilitaries or the guerrillas. a stick of dynamite exploded in the middle of the church, at the hour of the Elevation, with half the town inside; it was the first mass of Holy Thursday and there were fourteen dead and sixty-four wounded – the child was saved by a miracle: she was at the school selling little sugar figures; since then – some two years ago – she has lived and worked in the Brazilian's house on the recommendation of Father Albornoz. Very well instructed by Geraldina, she learned how to make all the meals, and lately was even concocting new dishes, so for the past year, at least, Geraldina has had no more to do with the kitchen. This I knew, seeing Geraldina tanning herself in the morning sun. drinking wine. stretched out with no concern other than the colour of her skin, the smell of her own hair as if it were the colour and texture of her heart. And not in vain when her long, long copper-coloured hair flew along every single street of this San José, town of peace, if she graced us with a stroll.

The diligent and still young Geraldina saved the money Gracielita earned.

"When you turn fifteen," I heard her say, "I shall

give you all the money you have earned and lots of presents as well. You can study dressmaking, you'll be a proper lady, you'll get married, we'll be the godparents of your first child, you'll come to see us every Sunday, won't you, Gracielita?" and she laughed, and I heard her, and Gracielita laughed too: in that house she had her own room, there awaiting her each night were her bed and her dolls.

We, their closest neighbours, could attest with hand on heart that they treated her just like a daughter.

At any time of the day the children would forget the world and play in the garden burning with light. I saw them. I heard them. They ran between the trees, rolled in each other's arms on the gentle grassy hillsides that stretched away from the house, dropped over the edges, and, after the game, after the hands that slipped together unnoticed, the necks and legs that brushed each other, the breath that intermingled, they went together to watch in fascination a leaping yellow frog or the surprising slither of a snake, which paralysed them with fear.

Sooner or later the shout would come from the terrace: it was Geraldina, more naked than ever, sinuous under the sun, her voice also a flame, sharp yet melodious.

She called: "Gracielita, time to sweep the hallway."

They left their game, and a slight sad annoyance returned them to the world. She went running at once back to the broom, across the garden, the white apron fluttering against her belly like a flag, hugging her young body, sculpting the pubis, but he followed her and soon enough took up again, involuntarily, not understanding, the other essential game, the paroxysm that made him identical to me, despite his youth, the panic game, the incipient but enthralling desire to look at her without her knowing, delectably to lie in wait for her: all of her a face in profile, her eyes as if absolved, steeped in who knows what dreams, then the calves, the round knees, the whole legs, just the thighs, and if he's lucky, beyond, up into the depths.

"You climb that wall every day, *profesor*. Don't you get bored?"

"No. I pick my oranges."

"And something more. You look at my wife."

The Brazilian and I studied each other for an instant.

"From what I can see," he said, "your oranges are round, but my wife must be more rounded, no?"

We smiled. What else could we do?

"It's true," I said. "If you say so."

I was not looking at his wife at that moment, only

5

at Gracielita, nevertheless, I glanced against my will towards the back of the patio where Geraldina, face down on the quilt, seemed to stretch. She raised arms and legs in every direction. I thought I saw an iridescent insect instead of her: suddenly she leapt to her feet, a resplendent grasshopper, but immediately she metamorphosed into nothing more and nothing less than a naked woman when she looked towards us, and began to walk in our direction, sure in her feline slowness, sometimes wrapped in the shade of the guayacan trees that grew by the house, grazed by the hundred-year-old branches of the cieba, sometimes as if consumed by the sun, which instead of shining brightly seemed to darken her with pure light, as if swallowing her. And that is how we watched her advance, just like a shadow.

Eusebio Almida, the Brazilian, had a bamboo cane in his hand and tapped it gently against his thick khaki riding trousers. He had just come back from hunting. Not far away I could hear his horse stamping the ground, between the sporadic chatter of the macaws. He saw that his wife was approaching, naked, skirting the tiles of the little round pool.

"I know very well," he said, smiling sincerely, "that it doesn't matter to her. That doesn't bother me. It's you I'm worried about, *profesor*, doesn't it hurt your heart? How many years old did you say you were?"

"All of them."

"You still have your sense of humour, that's for sure."

"What can I say?" I asked, looking at the sky: "I taught the man who is now mayor how to read, and Father Albornoz; I slapped both their wrists, and now you see, I wasn't wrong: we should be slapping them still."

"You make me laugh, *profesor*. Your way of changing the subject."

"What subject?"

But now his wife was with him, and with me, although she and I were separated by the wall, and time. Sweat glistened on her forehead. All of her smiled: the wide grin began in the sparse hair of the pink cleft in her centre that I sensed more than spied, up to the open mouth, with its small teeth, that laughed as if crying.

"Neighbour," she shouted festively, as she always did whenever we met on some street corner, "I'm so thirsty. Aren't you going to offer me an orange?"

There they were, happy, embracing now two metres below me, their young heads upturned and smiling, observing me as I did them. I chose the best orange and began to peel it myself, while they swayed together, amused. Neither she nor he seemed concerned about her nakedness. Only I was, but gave no sign of this solemn, inescapable emotion, as if never, in these last years of my life, had I suffered nor could I suffer from the nakedness of a woman. I stretched my arm down, the orange in my hand, towards her.

"Careful, *profesor*, don't fall," the Brazilian said. "Better throw that orange. I'll catch it."

But I kept leaning, outstretched, over the wall: she needed to take but one step and catch the orange. She half-opened her mouth, surprised, took the step and caught my orange, laughing again, enchanted.

"Thank you," she said.

A bitter and sweet fragrance rose from her reddened mouth. I know that same bittersweet exaltation struck us both.

"As you can see," the Brazilian said, "Geraldina doesn't mind being naked in your presence."

"And she's right," I said. "At my age I've seen everything now."

Geraldina laughed out loud: it was an unexpected flock of doves exploding at the edge of the wall. But she also looked at me with great curiosity, as if she had just for the first time discovered me in the world. I did not mind. She would have to discover me one day. She seemed to blush, for a moment only, and then she was disenchanted, or calmed, or perhaps she took pity. My old man's face, my future corpse, my saintliness in old age, quietened her. She did not yet perceive that my nostrils and my whole spirit were dilating to take in the aromas of her body, a blending of soap and sweat and skin and inaccessible bone. She had the orange in her hands and was pulling it apart. Finally she lifted a section to her mouth, spent a second licking it, bit into it, then gobbled it up with pleasure, shining drops trickling over her lip.

"Isn't our neighbour a delight?" the Brazilian said to nobody.

She took a sharp breath. She looked amazed, but still ruler of the world. She smiled at the sun.

"He is," she said languidly. "He is."

And they moved away, arm in arm, to the edge of the shade, but then she stopped, after a long step, so that now she looked at me with open legs, the sun converging in the centre, and cried out – the call of a rare bird.

"Thank you for the orange, kind sir."

She did not call me neighbour.

As she spoke, she had in that half-second already sensed that I was not looking into her eyes. She discovered suddenly, my gaze drawn, like a whirlpool of cloudy water, full of who knows what powers – she would have thought – my suffering eyes furtively glanced downwards, to her revealed core, her other mouth on

9

the verge of her most intimate voice: "Look at me, then," shouted her other voice, and shouted it despite my age, or probably, because of it: "Look at me, if you dare."

I am old, but not so old as to go unnoticed, I thought, as I climbed down the ladder. My wife was waiting for me with two glasses of lemonade – her way of saying good morning. But she looked me over with a somewhat haughty sadness.

"I knew they would make fun of you one of these days," she said. "Looking over there every morning, aren't you ashamed?"

"No," I said. "What should I be ashamed of?"

"Of yourself, at your time of life."

We drank our lemonade in silence. We did not talk about the fish or the cats as we usually do, or about the oranges, more of which we gave away than sold. We did not pick any flowers, the new blooms, we did not discuss possible changes in the garden, which is our life. We went straight to the kitchen and had breakfast, each absorbed in our own thoughts; in any case the black coffee, the soft-boiled egg, the slices of fried plantain absolved us of grief.

"Actually," she said at last, "I'm not worried about you, since I've known you for forty years. Or them. There's no hope for you three. But the children? What is that lady doing, walking around naked in front of her son, in front of poor little Gracielita? What kind of example are they setting?"

"The children don't see her," I said. "They walk right past her as if they really do not see her. Whenever she takes her clothes off, and he sings, the children play at her side. They're simply used to it."

"You don't miss a trick, do you? I think you ought to ask for help. From Father Albornoz, for example."

"Help?" I was shocked. And worse still: "Father Albornoz."

"I hadn't given a thought to your obsessions, but I think at your age they're detrimental. The Father could listen to you and help you, better than I could. To me, to tell you the truth, you don't matter any more. My fish and my cats matter more to me than a pitiful old man."

"But Father Albornoz," I laughed in amazement. "My former pupil. To whom I have myself confessed."

And I went back to bed to read the paper.

*

Like me, my wife is a teacher, also retired: the Secretary of Education owes us each ten months' worth of pension payments. She taught in a school in San Vicente – she was born and raised there, a town six hours from this one, where I was born. I met her in San Vicente, forty years ago, in the bus terminal, which in those days was an enormous corrugated-zinc shed. There I saw her, surrounded by sacks of fruit and orders of cornbread, dogs, pigs and hens, amid the exhaust of the motors and the prowling of the passengers waiting for their buses to leave. I saw her sitting alone on a wrought-iron bench, with room for two. I was dazzled by her dreamy black eyes, her wide forehead, her narrow waist, the ample backside under a pink skirt. The white, short-sleeved, linen blouse showed off her fine, pale arms and the intense darkness of her nipples. I went over and sat down beside her, as if levitating, but she immediately stood up, pretended to fix her hair, gave me a sidelong glance and walked away, feigning interest in the notices outside the transport office. Then something happened which distracted my attention from her uncommon rustic beauty; only such an incident could wrench my eyes from her: on the next bench was a much older man, rather fat, dressed in white; his hat was white too, as was the handkerchief poking out from behind his lapel; he was eating ice cream – just as white – clearly anxious;

the colour white was stronger than my love at first sight: too much white, also the thick drops of sweat soaking his bullish neck; all of him trembled, and that was in spite of being directly beneath the fan; his hefty body took up the whole bench, he was sprawled out, absolute master of his world; on the fingers of each hand he wore silver rings; there was a leather briefcase beside him, overflowing with documents; he gave the impression of total innocence: his blue eyes wandered distractedly all over the place: sweet and calm, they looked me over once but did not give me a second glance. And then another man, exactly the opposite, young and bone-jutting thin, barefoot, in a T-shirt and frayed shorts, walked up to him, put a revolver to his forehead and pulled the trigger. The cloud of smoke from the barrel was enough to envelop me; it was like a dream for everyone, including the fat man, who blinked and, at the moment of the shot, looked as though he still wanted to enjoy his ice cream. The one with the revolver fired only once; the fat man slid to one side, without falling, his eyes closed, as if he had all of a sudden fallen asleep, abruptly dead, but without letting go of his ice cream; the murderer threw the gun far away – a gun that no-one made any attempt to look for or pick up – and walked unhurriedly out of the bus station, without anyone stopping him. Except that a few seconds before throwing the gun away he looked at me, the fat man's nearest neighbour: never before in my life had I been struck by such a dead look; it was as if someone made of stone were looking at me: his gaze made me think he was going to shoot at me until he had emptied the chamber. And that was when I saw: the murderer was not a young man at all; he must have been no more than eleven or twelve. He was a child. I never knew if they followed him or caught him, and I never tried to find out; after all it was not so much his look that nauseated me: it was the physical horror of discovering that he was a child. A child, and that must have been why I was more afraid, and with reason, but also without reason, that he would kill me too. I fled from him, from where he had been, hunted for the bus station toilet, not yet knowing whether to piss or vomit, while the cry went up all about. Several men gathered round the corpse, no-one decided to give chase to the murderer: either we were all afraid, or it did not really seem to matter to anyone. I went into the lavatory: it was a small space with broken opaque mirrors, and at the back, the only cubicle looked like a crate – also made of corrugated-zinc sheets, like the terminal itself. I went and pushed the door and saw her just as she was sitting down, her dress bunched up around her waist, two thighs as pale as they were naked narrowing in terror. I said an anguished and heartfelt "Pardon me" and immediately closed the door at a speed calculated to allow me to take another look at her, the implacable roundness of her rump bursting out from under the hitched up skirt, her near nudity, her eyes – a rumble of fear and surprise and a hint of remote pleasure in the light of her pupils at knowing herself admired; of that I am now sure. And fate: we were assigned adjoining seats on the dilapidated bus that would take us to the capital. A long trip, more than eighteen hours, awaited us: the pretext to listen to each other was the death of the fat man in white in the terminal; I felt her arm brush against my arm, but also all of her fear, her indignation, the whole heart of the woman who would be my wife. And the coincidence: we shared the same profession, who could have imagined? Two educators, forgive me for asking, what is your name? (silence), my name is Ismael Pasos, and you? (silence), she was only listening, but finally: "My name is Otilia del Sagrario Aldana Ocampo." The same hopes. Soon the murder and the incident in the toilet were forgotten – but only apparently, because they went on recurring, becoming associated, in an almost absurd way, in my memory: first death, then nakedness.

Today my wife, ten years younger than me, is sixty, but she looks older, she moans and walks hunched over.

She is not the same girl she was at twenty sitting down on a public toilet, her eyes like lighthouse beams over the hitched up island, the join of her legs, the triangle of her sex – indescribable animal – no. Now she is old, happy indifference, going from here to there, in the middle of her country and its war, busy with her house, the cracks in the walls, the possible leaks in the roof, although the shouts of the war burst in her ears, she is just like everyone, when it comes right down to it, and I am happy for her happiness, and if she loved me today as much as she does her fish and her cats perhaps I would not be peering over the wall.

Perhaps.

"From the first time I met you," she says that night at bedtime, "you've never stopped spying on women. I would have left you forty years ago if I thought you would take things any further. But no."

I listen to her sigh: I think I can see it, it is a vapour rising in the middle of the bed, covering us both.

"You were and are just a naïve, inoffensive peeping Tom."

Now I sigh. Is it resignation? I do not know. And I shut my eyes tight, and nevertheless listen to her.

"At first it was difficult, I suffered from knowing that apart from spying on women you spent the days of your life teaching boys and girls to read at school. Who could imagine? But I kept an eye out, and I repeat this was just at the beginning, for I saw you never really got up to anything serious, nothing bad or sinful that we would live to regret. At least that's what I believed, or wanted to believe, for heaven's sake."

The silence can also be seen, like the sigh. It is yellow, it slips through the pores of the skin like fog, it climbs up the window.

"That hobby of yours made me sad," she says as if smiling. "But I soon got used to it: I forgot about it for years at a time. And why did I forget? Because you used to be very careful not to be seen; I was the only witness. Well, remember when we lived in that red building in Bogotá. You spied on the woman in the building opposite, day and night, until her husband found out, remember. He shot at you from the other room, and you told me yourself that the bullet parted your hair. What if he had killed you, that husband, that man of honour?"

"We wouldn't have a daughter," I said. And I dared, finally, to surrender: "I think I'm going to go to sleep."

"Tonight you're not going to go to sleep, Ismael; for so many years you've been going to sleep every time I want to talk. Tonight you're not going to ignore me."

"No."

"I'm telling you at least to be discreet. I have to point it out to you, as old as you may be. What just happened is degrading to you, and degrading to me. I heard the whole thing; I'm not deaf, as you seem to think."

"You're a spy too, in your own way"

"Yes. Spying on the spy. You're not discreet, as you used to be. I've seen you in the street. Ismael, you practically drool. I thank heaven that our daughter and our grandchildren live far away and don't see you at it. How shameful with the Brazilian, with his wife. Let them do what they like, it's fine, we are each master of our own flesh and its corruption; but for them to find you up a ladder like a sick man spying on them is a shame that applies to me too. Promise me that you won't climb up there again."

"And the oranges? Who's going to pick the oranges?"

"I've already thought of that. But it won't be you, not any more."

Every 9 March, for the last four years, we have been visiting Hortensia Galindo. On that day many of her friends help her to endure the disappearance of her husband, Marcos Saldarriaga, whom no-one knows whether God has in his Glory, or his Gloria has in hers – as the wagging tongues have begun to joke, referring to Saldarriaga's mistress, Gloria Dorado.

We gather at dusk. We ask about his fate and the reply is always the same: *nothing is known*. In their house – friends, acquaintances and strangers – we drink rum. On the long concrete patio, where there are many hammocks and rocking chairs, a crowd of young people, including Saldarriaga's twin sons, make the most of the occasion. Inside the house we old folks cluster round Hortensia and listen to her. She does not cry now, as she used to; perhaps she is resigned, but who knows? She does not behave like a widow: she says her husband is still alive and that God will help him find his way back to his loved ones. She must be forty or so, although she looks younger: she is young in spirit and in appearance, fleshy, more than exuberant, grateful for the company on the melancholy anniversary of her husband's disappearance, and she gives thanks in an unusual way: when she says *Thank God* her open, trembling hands touch her breasts – two colossal round melons. Maybe I am the only one to witness this gesture, which she repeats each year: perhaps she seeks merely to point out her heart: who will ever know? Two years ago they even had music in the house and, whether God willed it or not, people seemed to forget the fearful fate that every disappearance is, and even the possible death of the one who is missing. People forget everything, good heavens, and the young especially, who have no memory even of today; that is why they are almost happy.

Because the last time there was dancing.

"Let them dance," Hortensia Galindo said, coming out to the lighted patio, where the young people were happily switching partners. "Marcos would like it. He always was, and *is*, a joyful man. The best party will be the day he comes home."

That was last year, and Father Albornoz left,

extremely annoyed by her decision.

"So he could be alive, or he could be dead," he said, "but either way, there has to be dancing." And he left the house.

He could not have heard, nor did he want to hear, Hortensia Galindo's reply.

"Even if he is dead: it was on the dance floor that I fell in love with him."

We do not know if after what happened Father Albornoz will want to call on Hortensia Galindo today. Possibly not. My wife and I wonder as we cross the town. Hortensia's house is on the far side from ours, and, arm in arm, we encourage each other to walk, or rather, she encourages me; the only exercise I take these days is climbing the ladder, stretching as far as I can, as if on a vertical bed, and collecting the oranges from the trees of my orchard; it is enjoyable exercise, un-hurried, that suits me in the morning hours – what with all there is to look at.

Walking has become torture for me of late: my left knee hurts, my feet swell; but I do not complain in front of others, as my wife does, of varicose veins. Nor do I want to use a walking stick; I do not go to see Dr Orduz because I am sure he would prescribe a stick, and I associate sticks with death and have done since

I was a boy: the first dead man I saw, as a child, was my grandfather, leaning against his avocado tree, his head drooping, straw hat covering half his face, and a walking stick made from a guayacan branch between his knees, his stiff hands fastened to the handle. I thought he was asleep, but soon I heard my grandmother crying: "So you've finally died and left me, tell me what should I do now, die myself?"

"Listen," I say to Otilia. "I want to think about what you said last night. You've made me ashamed to face people, what was that about me drooling in the streets? No, don't answer. I'd rather be by myself for a few minutes. I'm going to drink a cup of coffee at Chepe's and I'll catch you up."

She stops walking and stares at me open-mouthed.

"Do you feel alright?"

"I've never felt better. It's just that I don't want to go to Hortensia's yet. I'll be there soon."

"Good that you've learned your lesson," she says. "But it's not the end of the world."

Right where we are, on the corner of the street, is Chepe's café. It is five in the afternoon and the tables – the ones near the pavement – are empty still. I make for one of those tables. My wife does not move: she is a white dress with red flowers in the middle of the road.

23

"I'll wait for you there," she says. "Don't be long. It's bad manners for a couple to come calling at separate times."

And she goes on her way.

I take hold of the nearest chair, drop into it. My knee is boiling inside. "Oh, God," I sigh to myself, "I'm still here only because I have been incapable of killing myself."

"What music would you like to hear, *profesor*?"

Chepe has emerged from his shop, and brings me a beer.

"Whatever music you prefer, Chepe, and I don't want beer, thank you, bring me a coffee good and black, please."

"Why the long face, *profesor*? It bores you to visit Hortensia? The food is good there, is it not?"

"Tired, Chepe, tired from a short walk. I promised to join Otilia in ten minutes."

"Well then, I'm going to bring you a coffee so black you won't be able to sleep."

But he puts the beer down on the table.

"Compliments of the house."

Despite the cooling afternoon, the other pain, the one within, persists in burning my knee: all the heat of the earth seems to take refuge there. I drink half the beer, but the fire in my knee has become so unbearable that, after making sure Chepe is not keeping an eye on me from behind the counter, I roll up my trouser leg and pour the rest of the beer over my knee. Even this does nothing for the burning. "I'll have to go and see Orduz," I say to myself, resigned.

It begins to get dark; the street lights come on: yellow and weak, they produce large shadows, as if instead of illuminating they darken. I do not know how long a table next to mine has been occupied by two ladies; two chattery birds that I remember, two ladies who were once my pupils. And they see that I see them.

"*Profesor*," says one of them.

I reply to her greeting by bowing my head.

"*Profesor*," she repeats.

I recognize her, and I am going to remember: was it her? When she was a little girl, at primary school, behind the dusty schoolyard cacao trees, I saw her hitch up the skirt of her uniform and show herself split in the middle to a little boy, barely a step away, possibly more frightened than she was, both of them blushing and stupefied; I didn't say anything to them: how could I have interrupted them? I wonder what Otilia would have done in my place.

The women are old now, though quite a bit younger than Otilia; they were my pupils, I remind myself, flaunting my memory, I identify them: *Rosita Viterbo, Ana*

Cuenco. Now each of them has more than five children, at least. The boy who was disturbed by Rosita's charm, the hitching up of her skirt, was it not Emilio Forero? Always solitary, he was not yet twenty when he was killed, in the street, by a stray bullet, without anyone knowing who, where from, how.

They greet me with affection.

"How hot it was at midday, wasn't it, *profesor*?"

I do not respond, however, to their apparent appeal for a chat; I go on as if I had not heard: let them think me senile. Beauty overwhelms, dazzles: I could never keep from averting my eyes from the eyes of the beauty who looks back, but the mature woman, like these who brush hands as they talk, or the women full of old age, or those ones who are much older than those full of age, tend to be only good or great friends, faithful confidantes, wise advisers. They do not inspire my compassion (any more than I inspire it), or love either (any more than I inspire it). Someone young and unknown is always more bewitching.

That is what I am thinking – like an invocation – when I hear someone call me "sir" and the air beside me is permeated by the musky draught of the slender Geraldina, accompanied by her son and Gracielita. They sit down at my pupils' table; Geraldina orders curuba juice for everyone, greets the ladies warmly, questions

26

them, they reply yes, we too are going to Hortensia's house, and we are here – adds Ana Cuenco – because look what a fine example the teacher sets, as soon as we saw him we felt like keeping him company while he had a rest.

"Thanks for that," I say. "All the same, when I die will you keep me company?"

Unanimous and sing-song laughter surrounds me: more than feminine, it slips through the air, crosses the night: what forest am I in, with little birds?

"Don't be a pessimist, sir" – Geraldina is speaking, and everything seems to indicate that she will never again call me neighbour – "maybe we'll die first."

"Never. God would not commit such an error."

The ladies nod their agreement, with solemn and grateful smiles; Geraldina opens her mouth, as if she wanted to say something and changed her mind.

Chepe arrives with the curuba juice; he leaves me a steaming cup of coffee. Geraldina sighs tumultuously – as if at the peak of lovemaking – and asks for an ashtray. It is a miracle, this presence; it is a potion; Geraldina is a remedy: now I feel no burning in my knee, the tiredness in my feet disappears, I could run.

I spy on her from here: without resting on the back of her chair, knees together but calves apart, very slowly, delicately, she removes her sandals, leans her body even further: revealing her neck, which is like a mast; the children greet their curuba juice voluptuously: their lips slurp, noisily, thirstily, while the night shines around them and I raise my cup and pretend to sip my coffee; Geraldina, naked the morning before, is dressed this evening: a vaporous little lavender frock undresses her another way, or undresses her more, you might say; she redeems me dressed or with her nakedness, if she is naked her other nakedness, the last glimpse of her sex, if only her remotest fold opening as she walks, all the dancing in her back, heart beating solemnly in her chest, in the shape of her bottom, her soul; I ask nothing more of life than this possibility, to see this woman without her knowing that I'm looking at her, to see this woman when she knows I'm looking, but to see her: my only explanation for staying alive. She leans back in the chair, lifts one leg over the other and lights a cigarette, only she and I know that I am looking at her, and meanwhile my former pupils go on with their prattle, what are they saying? Impossible to listen, the children finish their curuba juice, ask permission to order more and disappear hand in hand into the shop, I know they do not want ever to return, that if it were up to them they would flee hand in hand to the furthest night of time, now again Geraldina uncrosses her legs, leans towards me, imperceptible, studies me, just for one second her eyes like a veiled warning touch me and confirm that I am definitely still looking at her, perhaps she is startled by such disproportionate, monstrous frankness, that someone, I, at my age, but what to do? All of her is the most intimate desire because I look at her, I admire her, the same as the rest of them look at her, admire her, much younger than me, the little boys – yes, she shouts, and I hear her, she wants to be looked at, admired, pursued, caught, turned over, bitten and licked, killed, revived and killed again for generations.

Again I hear the ladies' voices. Geraldina has let out a little cry of sincere astonishment. For an instant her knees part, looking yellow under the street lights; her thighs, scarcely concealed by her short summer dress, appear. I take the last sip of my coffee: I distinguish, without managing to hide the fact, in the depths of Geraldina, the bulging little triangle, but the dazzle is spoilt by my ears, which struggle to confirm my former pupils' words; they clamour about the horrible discovery of the corpse of a newborn this morning, at the rubbish dump, are they really saying that?

Yes, they repeat: "They killed a newborn baby girl," and cross themselves. "Chopped into pieces. God help us."

Geraldina bites her lips.

"They could have left her at the church door, alive," she moans – what a beautifully candid voice – and asks of the heavens: "Why kill her?"

That is how they are talking, and, suddenly, one of my pupils – Rosita Viterbo? – who I never noticed watching me watch Geraldina (surely because my wife is right and I no longer manage the discretion of years gone by: am I drooling? God, I shout wordlessly at myself: Rosita Viterbo saw me suffering at the vision of the two open thighs showing infinity inside), Rosita stroking her cheek with one finger and addressing me with mild sarcasm, says: "And what do you think, *profesor*?"

"It's not the first time," I manage to say. "Not in this town, nor in the country."

"I'm sure it's not," says Rosita. "Nor in the world. That we already know."

"Many children, as I recall, have been killed by their mothers after birth; and they always alleged the same thing: it was to save them from the world's misery."

"That's horrible what you say, *profesor*," Ana Cuenco rebels. "How despicable, and I beg your pardon, but that does not explain, much less justify, the death of any newborn baby."

"I never claimed it justified it," I defend myself, and

I see that Geraldina has closed her knees again; she stubs the cigarette out on the dirt floor, ignoring the ashtray, runs her two long hands over her hair, which she wears up today, and exhales listlessly, surely appalled by the conversation, or weary?

"What a world," she says.

The children, her children, come back to her, one on each side, as if protecting her, without knowing exactly what from. Geraldina pays Chepe and stands up stricken, as if under an enormous weight – the inexplicable conscience of an inexplicable country, I say to myself, a burden of a little less than two hundred years which nonetheless does not keep her from stretching her whole body, lifting her breasts beneath her dress, sketching an uncertain smile, as if licking her lips.

"But let's go to Hortensia's," she pleads with a wail. "It's dark already."

And Rosita Viterbo, my one-time pupil, watches me in a distracted way.

"Aren't you coming, *profesor*?"

"I'll come later," I say.

In short, I did not go to call on Hortensia Galindo this year.

I said goodbye to Chepe and turned at the next corner, on the way to Mauricio Rey's house. I have confused the streets and come out at the edge of town, darker and darker, strewn with filth and rubbish – some old, some new – a sort of cliff, which I peer over: it must be thirty years since I've been out here. What is it, what sparkles down there like a silver ribbon? The river. It used to rage all through the hellish summer, and it was a torrent. In this mountain town there is no sea, but there *was* a river. Today, desiccated by a pallid heat, it is a little meandering thread. That was another time when we used to go to the most abundant bends in its waters, in the middle of summer, not only to fish: naked and immersed up to their necks the girls smiled, whispered, floated, blurred, in the clear water. But later they sprang out more real and furtive, on tiptoes, looking from one side to the other, taking big steep jumps while they dried off and dressed, quickly, looking carefully every once in a while through the trees. Soon they relaxed, believing the world around them slept: only the song of a small owl, the song of my chest high up in an orange tree, the heart of every adolescent boy in town watching them. Because there were trees for all.

There is no sign of a moon, occasionally a street light, there is no living shadow in the streets, the gathering at Hortensia Galindo's house is quite an event, as if the war had arrived in the plaza, in the school, at your door, when the whole town hides.

To get to Rey's house I have to return to Chepe's and from there restart the route — as if the past could be restarted. I have to remember: the house was the last one along a dirt road, near an abandoned guitar workshop: then came the cliff. The sleepy-looking girl who opens the door tells me that Mauricio is sick in bed, that he cannot see anyone.

"Who is it?" Mauricio Rey's voice comes from inside.

"It's me."

"*Profesor*, what an unexpected pleasure! Will miracles never cease? You know the way here."

Whose is this girl? I seem to see her and not see her.

"Whose daughter are you?"

"Sultana's."

"I know Sultana. She was rather naughty, but she studied. Do you know me?"

"You're the schoolteacher."

"*Profesor Pasos, we used to say,*" Rey shouts from his room, "*why does he always fail us?*"

He is the oldest of my pupils, and one of my few friends now. There, in his bed, a bearded sixty-year-old, under the yellow light from the bare bulb, he laughs, more toothless than me: he doesn't have his bridge in, is he not embarrassed with this girl? For the last four years, he told me once, when the commemoration takes place and his wife – his second wife, because he is a widower – goes to offer her condolences for the disappearance of Saldarriaga, he has pretended to be ill and stayed at home and done with the girl who happened to be there what he could not do the whole year long.

"So, what news?" he asks. "I was thinking about the party, *profesor.*"

"What party, if you please?"

"The celebration, for Saldarriaga."

"Celebration?"

"Celebration, *profesor*, and forgive me, but that Saldarriaga was, or is, if he's alive, a triple son of a bitch."

"I haven't come to talk about that."

"What then, *profesor*, don't you see I'm pressed for time?"

The truth is that I do not myself know why I have come: what am I going to invent? Is it this girl? Have I come here to meet this girl with her hair so recently messed?

"My knee hurts," it occurs to me to tell Rey.

"It's old age, *profesor*," he roars. "What do you think you are, immortal?"

He is drunk, I realize. At his side, scattered on the floor, are two or three aguardiente bottles.

"I thought you just pretended to be ill," I say, pointing to the bottles.

He laughs and offers me a glass, which I refuse.

"Go, *profesor*."

"You're throwing me out?"

"Go to Maestro Claudino's place, and tell me about it later. He'll fix your knee."

"Is he still alive?"

"Say hello to him from me, *profesor*."

The girl accompanies me to the door: sumptuous in her innocence, unbuttoning her blouse to save time.

I was still a boy when I met Claudino Alfaro. He is alive, then. If I am seventy, he must be a hundred, or close to it. Why did I forget about him? Why did he forget about me? Instead of entrusting myself to Ordúz, the doctor, Mauricio Rey reminded me of Maestro Claudino, who I had long given up for more than dead, since I didn't even remember him. Where have I existed these years? I answer myself: up on the wall, peering over.

And I leave the town, unwary beneath the night, walking to the cabin of Maestro Claudino, folk healer. The pain in my knee, again, urges me on.

He is alive, so, he is alive, like me, I say to myself, as I walk down the road. The last lights of the town disappear with the first bend, the night grows larger, with no stars. He will go on living while he heals: he makes his patients urinate into a bottle, then he shakes the bottle, and reads, against the light, the sicknesses; he straightens out muscles, sticks bones back together. "He is as alive as I believe I am," I say to myself, and climb Chuzo's mountain, following the bridle path. I must have stopped several times to rest. The last time I admit defeat and decide to go back; I suddenly discover that I have to drag my leg to make any progress at all. This outing was a mistake, I say to myself, but I walk uphill, from stone to stone. At a bend in the path, already in the invisible jungle of the mountain, I give up and look for a place to rest. There is no moon, the night is still pitch black; I cannot see a pace in front of me, although I know I am halfway there: the Maestro's cabin is at the back of the mountain, not at its summit, which today I would never reach, but rather skirting round halfway up. I find a mound finally, and sit down there. Above my knee the swelling has grown to the size of an orange. I am drenched in sweat, as if caught in the rain; there is no wind, and, nevertheless, I hear that something or someone is walking on and snapping the leaves and underbrush. I freeze. I try to distinguish between the shapes of the bushes. The noise approaches; what if it is an attack? It could be that the guerrillas, or the paramilitaries, have decided to take the town tonight, why not? Captain Berrío must be at Hortensia's house, the guest of honour. The noises stop for an instant. Expectation makes me forget the pain in my knee. I am far from town, no-one can hear me. They will probably shoot first and, then, when I am already dying, come and see me and ask who I am – if I am still alive. But they could also be soldiers, training at night, I tell myself, to calm down. "All the same," I shout at myself, "they'll shoot me just the same." And, at that, with an explosion of leaves and stalks parting, I perceive something, or someone, leaping upon me. I scream. I reach out my arms, hands open, to repel the attack, the blow, the ghost, whatever it is. I know that this gesture is of no use, and I think of Otilia: Tonight you will not find me in bed. I do not know how long I have my eyes closed. Something touches my shoes, sniffs me. An enormous dog puts his paws on my lap, stretches, and now licks my face in greeting. "It's a dog," I say aloud. "It's just a dog, thank God," and I do not know if I am going to laugh or cry: as if I still love life.

"Who's that? Who's there?"

The voice is just the same: a husky wind, elongated.

"Who's there?"

"It's me. Ismael."

"Ismael Pasos. Then you're not dead."

"I don't think so."

So we were thinking the same thing: that the other was dead.

I can only see him when he is a step away from me. He is wearing a sort of sheet around his waist; he still has his hair like little tufts of cotton; I can just make out his gleaming eyes in the night; I wonder if he can distinguish my eyes, or if only his eyes shine through the black night. The incomprehensible fear he caused me as a child returns again, fleetingly, but fear it was; I stand up and feel his hand on my arm, like wire, as thin and as tight.

He holds me up.

"What's the matter?" he says. "Does your leg hurt?"

"My knee."

"Let's see."

Now his wiry hands brush my knee.

"This had to happen for you to come to see me, Ismael. One more day and you wouldn't be able to walk. Now we have to get the swelling down, for a start. Let's go on up."

He wants to help me walk up the hill. I am embarrassed. He must be close to a hundred.

"I can still manage."

"Up you go, let's see."

The dog goes ahead of us; I hear him run, uphill, while I drag my leg.

"I thought they were going to kill me," I tell him. "I thought it was the war coming down on me."

"You thought your time had come."

"Yes. I thought I was dead."

"That's what I thought four years ago."

His voice moves away, like his story.

"It was already late and I was in the hammock, taking off my shoes, when they appeared.

"'Come with us,' they said.

"I told them I didn't mind, whenever they wanted,

I told them all I asked was a bit of sugar-water in the mornings.

"'Don't complain,' they told me. 'We'll give or not give you whatever we feel like, depending on our mood.'

"That was a brutal walk; at full speed, as if the soldiers were closing in on them.

"'And this one, who is he? Why did we bring him?' one of them said.

"*None of them know me*, I thought, and I didn't know any one of them either, I'd never seen them in my life; their accents were from Antioquia; they were young and they climbed; I kept up with their pace, of course. They wanted to get rid of my dog, who was following us.

"'Don't shoot him,' I said. 'He obeys me. Tony, go home,' I begged more than ordered him, pointing down the path towards the cabin, and this blessed Tony obeyed, lucky for him."

"This same dog?"

"This one."

"An obedient dog."

"That was four years ago, the same day they took Marcos Saldarriaga."

"Who could have imagined it, the very same day? No-one told me that."

"Because I never told anyone, to stay out of trouble."

"Of course."

"After walking all night, when it was starting to get light, we stopped in that place they call the Three Crosses."

"They took you that far?"

"And I saw him there, sitting on the ground, Marcos Saldarriaga. They took him further, not me."

"And how was he, what did he say?"

"He didn't even recognize me."

Maestro Claudino's voice is pained:

"He was crying. Remember he is, or was, pretty fat, twice the size of his wife. He just couldn't go on. They were looking for a mule to carry him. There was a woman as well: Carmina Lucero, the baker, remember her? From San Vicente, Otilia's town. Otilia must know her, how is Otilia?"

"The same."

"That means she's still well. The last time I saw her was at the market. She was buying leeks, how did she cook them?"

"I don't remember."

"They took the baker too, poor thing."

"Carmina?"

"Carmina Lucero. Someone told me she died in captivity, after two years. I still didn't know who they were, whether they were guerrillas or paras. Nor did I ask them.

41

"The one in charge reprimanded the boys.

"He said: 'Morons, what did you bring this old guy for? Who the fuck is he?'

"'They say he's a healer,' one of them said.

"*So they do know me, I thought.*

"'Healer?' the one in charge yelled. 'What he wants is a doctor.'

"'He?' I thought. 'Who is he?' Must be someone in charge of the one in charge.

"But at that moment I heard the one in charge tell them: 'Get rid of this old man.'

"And when he said *Get rid of this old man* a boy put the muzzle of his rifle to the back of my neck. That's when I felt as you did a little while ago, Ismael."

"That I was dead."

"Thank God I still had the strength to be grateful that it wasn't a machete on my neck, instead of that rifle. How many have they just slashed without even giving them a *coup de grâce* afterwards?"

"Almost all of them."

"All of them, Ismael."

"It must be better to die of a gunshot than by machete. How was it they didn't kill you?"

"The one in charge said to the boy: 'I didn't tell you to kill him, idiot.' He said that, thank God. 'He's so old he'll save us a bullet, or the effort,' he said. 'Get lost.'

"'In any event,' I answered him, and I still don't know why I opened my mouth, 'if I can help in some way, I won't have come all this way for nothing. Who needs curing?'

"'Nobody, old man. Get lost.' And they kicked me out.

"I was starting to find my way, to come home, when they ordered me to return. Now the boys took me to where the ill man was, the real big boss. He was some way off, lying in a tent. A girl, in military uniform, on her knees, was cutting his toenails.

"'So?' the boss said when he saw me arrive. 'You're the healer.'

"'Yes, sir.'

"'And how do you heal?'

"'Tell them to bring an empty bottle, and urinate in it. There I'll see.'

"'The boss burst out laughing. But a moment later he became serious.'

"'Take this skeleton away,' he shouted. 'What I can't do is piss, for fuck's sake.'

"I wanted to propose a different remedy, now that I knew what was wrong, but the man gestured with his hand and the girl who had been cutting his nails pushed me out of the tent with the butt of her rifle."

"And they put a gun to you again?"

"No," the Maestro's voice turned bitter. "The boss missed his chance for help."

"And what happened to Marcos Saldarriaga?"

"He stayed there, crying, and him such a proud man. It was pitiful. You couldn't help but notice, not even the woman from the bakery was crying."

I stopped. I wished I could do away with my leg. I wanted to be rid of that pain.

"Up, up, Ismael," the Maestro said to me laughing. "We're almost there."

The cabin at last appeared around a corner, the light of a candle flickering in the only window, just when I was going to collapse on the ground, sleep, die, forget, whatever, anything not to feel my knee. He made me lie down in the hammock and went into the kitchen. I could see him. He put some roots on the stove to boil. I touched my face: I thought I was sweating from the heat. It was not the heat. At that hour, on the mountain – one of the highest in the range – it was cold. I had a fever. The dog would not let me sleep, he licked the sweat from my hands, put his paw on my chest; I'd catch sight of his eyes like two sparkling flames. The Maestro put a poultice on my knee and tied it in place with a strip of cloth.

"Now we have to wait," he said, "an hour, at least. Does Otilia know you came up here?"

"No."

"Oh, she's going to scold you, Ismael."

And he gave me a gourd of cane liquor to drink.

"It's strong," I said. "I'd rather have coffee."

"Absolutely not. You have to drink it, so your soul will sleep and you won't feel anything."

"I'll be drunk."

"No. You're just going to have a waking sleep, but you must drink it down in one gulp, not in little sips."

With trust I drank the contents of the gourd. I do not know how much time passed, nor when the pain disappeared, along with the swelling. Maestro Claudino squatted, looking at the night. His old *tiple* guitar was hanging on one of the walls. The dog had gone to sleep, curled up at his feet.

"It doesn't hurt any more," I said. "I can go now."

"No, Ismael. The best is yet to come."

And he brought a stool up beside the hammock and made me stretch out my leg to rest on it. Then he stood astride my leg, but without putting any weight on it, just pinning it between his knees.

"Bite on a piece of your shirt, if you want, Ismael, so you won't hear yourself scream," and I shuddered, remembering his cures, which I had witnessed on

45

occasion, but never experienced in my own flesh: dislocated elbows, necks, ankles, fingers, thrown-out backs, broken legs, and I remembered how his patients had screamed, how the walls had rocked.

As soon as I had clenched the sleeve of my shirt in my teeth his wiry fingers alighted on my knee like birds' talons, felt around, recognized it and, all of a sudden, squeezed, grabbing the bone or the bones and I do not know when or how they opened and closed the knee, as if putting together the pieces of that puzzle of bone and cartilage that was my knee, that was me, worse than the dentist, I got as far as thinking, and though I bit the shirt I could hear my scream.

"That's it."

I looked at him stunned, trembling with fever.

"I should have another shot of liquor."

"No."

The pain had disappeared, there was no pain. Very gingerly I began to lower myself out of the hammock and, still not believing it, stood up and put weight on my leg. Nothing. No pain. I walked, from here to there, from there to here.

"It's a miracle," I said.

"No. It's me."

I felt like running, like a foal finally standing up.

"You still have to take it easy, Ismael. You have to

let it rest for three days, for the bones to set. Try to go down slowly, don't be foolhardy."

"How much do I owe you, Maestro," and, again, I did not know if I was going to cry or laugh.

"Bring a hen, when you're quite better. It's been a long time since I've tasted a chicken stew, since I've talked to a friend."

I took my time going down the bridle path. No pain. I turned round to look: Maestro Claudino and his dog were standing there watching me. I waved goodbye, and went on.

She was waiting for me, sitting in her chair by the front door. It was after midnight and there were no lights on.

"Sooner or later you were bound to come back," she said.

"How was it, Otilia? What did I miss?"

"Everything."

She did not even ask me where I had been. Nor did I wish to talk about Maestro Claudino and my knee. She turned on the light in the bedroom and we lay down on the bed, on top of the covers. She had given me a plate of stuffed pork and a cup of coffee.

"So you don't fall asleep," she said. And explained: "Hortensia Galindo sent you the pork. I had to make excuses for you, say you weren't well, that your legs were hurting you."

"My left knee." And I began to eat hungrily.

48

"Father Albornoz didn't go," she told me. "He didn't go to Hortensia's. And nobody cared. The mayor arrived without his wife, without his children, Dr Orduz, Captain Berrío, Mauricio Rey, drunk but calm."

"And the youngsters? Did the young people have a party?"

"There was no party."

"Really? The girls didn't dance?"

"There wasn't a single girl on the patio. They've all gone in this past year."

"All of them?"

"All the girls and all the boys, Ismael." She gave me a reproachful look. "The most sensible thing they could do."

"It won't be any better elsewhere."

"They had to leave to find out."

Otilia went to the kitchen and came back with another cup of coffee. This time she did not lie down beside me. She drank her coffee and stared blindly out of the window. What could she see? It was night-time; we could hear only the cicadas.

"And *she* turned up," she said.

"Who?"

"Gloria Dorado."

I waited.

And eventually: "With a letter that she had received

from Marcos Saldarriaga two years ago; she turned up to say that she thought perhaps that letter would help to get him freed. And she put it on a table."

"On a table?"

"In front of Hortensia Galindo.

"'I cannot possibly read this,' said Hortensia as she picked it up. But she read out loud: *My name is Marcos Saldarriaga. I am writing this in my own hand.*"

"She read that?"

"'I recognize his handwriting,' Hortensia said."

"And? No-one said anything?"

"No-one. She just kept reading. It was as if she was listening herself, unable to believe it, but with no choice but to believe it. In that letter Marcos Saldarriaga asked Gloria Dorado, of all people, to make sure Hortensia was never allowed to take charge of his liberation. *Hortensia would like to see me dead*, Hortensia Galindo read out loud, her voice steady. She was strong enough to read it."

"Damn me."

"She was reading the words of a madman, that's what I thought, at first. Not even a madman would take it into his head to make so many enemies in such a way, starting with his wife. In that letter Marcos spoke ill of everyone, even Father Albornoz, whitewashed sepulchre, he called him, said that everyone wanted to

50

see him dead, from that hypocrite Mauricio Rey right the way down to the Mayor, betrayer of his people, by way of General Palacios, that bird breeder, he called him, and Dr Orduz: pig-headed quack. He begged Gloria Dorado not to let the people of his town negotiate his liberty, for the opposite would happen, they would do things backwards, and so backwards that sooner or later he would turn up dead at the side of a road."

"Well, he hasn't turned up yet, either dead or alive."

"And still Hortensia read, without her voice breaking: *Make this public, so the world will know the truth: they want to kill me, those who say they want to liberate me every bit as much as those who are holding me prisoner.* This last bit etched itself in my memory because that was when I realized that Marcos had already given himself up for dead, that he wasn't mad and that he was telling the truth, the truth that comes only from desperation, as told by one who knows his death is near, so why lie? The man who lies at the hour of his death is not a man."

"And no-one said anything? How could everybody keep quiet?"

"They all wanted to hear something worse."

We heard the buzzing of an insect in the room; it flew around the light bulb, crossed between our gazes, landed on the crucifix above the bed, then on the head of the old wooden Saint Anthony, a sort of altar in the corner, and finally flew away.

"I too am somewhat pleased, I confess, that Marcos Saldarriaga has disappeared," I dared to tell Otilia.

"There are things we should not say aloud, not even to those who love us most. They are the things that cause walls to listen, Ismael, understand?"

I laughed.

"Everyone knows those things, long before the walls do," I told her.

"But it is unforgivable to say them. This is a man's life."

"I am only saying what I think, which is what everyone thinks, although no-one in the world deserves that fate, that's cruel."

"There is no word for it," she said.

I began to undress, down to my underwear. She looked at me closely.

"What?" I said. "You like ruins?"

And I got under the covers and told her I wanted to sleep.

"That's what you're like," she said, "sleep, watch, and sleep. Don't you want to hear what Geraldina, your neighbour, did?"

I pretended to be unconcerned. But that shook me.

"What did she do?"

"She took her children and she left."

Otilia examined me much more closely.

"Before she left she had time to speak, oh yes."

"What did she say?"

"That it was a disgrace that Gloria Dorado, at this point, two years after receiving a letter, should turn up to hand it over, when it had nothing to do with anything any more. Marcos Saldarriaga's situation was very serious, she said, he was not in his right mind, who could be, held prisoner day and night, by people he doesn't even know, not knowing for how long, perhaps till his death? The things Marcos said were just private affairs, misunderstandings, matrimonial quarrels, desperation, and it was not wise to bring such a letter to a woman as distressed as Hortensia.

"'What he requested has been carried out,' Gloria Dorado interrupted her. 'It has been made public. For two years I didn't show anyone because the things he wrote seemed harsh, even unjust. But I see that I should have done so sooner, because it's very possible that what he says is true, that nobody here wants his freedom, not even Father Albornoz.'

"'You wicked woman!' shouted Hortensia Galindo. No-one knew when she had leapt towards Gloria, her hands out in front of her, as if she wanted to grab her by the hair, but she had the bad luck to trip and fall and bounce, fat as she is, at the feet of the Dorado woman, who shouted: "I'm sure that I am the only one in this town who wants to see Marcos Saldarriaga free, you criminals."

Ana Cuenco and Rosita Viterbo went to help Hortensia up. No man stepped forward; either they were more frightened than we were or they thought this was a women's matter.

"'Get out of my house,' Hortensia screamed, but the Dorado woman did not go. 'Didn't you hear? Get out,' Rosita Viterbo screamed, and the Dorado woman still did not move.

"Then Ana and Rosita jumped on her; they each grabbed an arm and took her to the patio door; once they were there they pushed her out and closed the door."

"They did?"

"All by themselves." Otilia sighed. "Thank God Gloria didn't turn up with her brother, who would not have allowed it. If a single man got involved, more would follow, and worse things would have happened."

"Like shots being fired."

"That's how stupid men are," she said staring hard at me and unable to help smiling. But a moment later her face froze. "How sad: Ana and Rosita began serving up the pork; Hortensia Galindo was in a terrible state, sitting in her chair, the plate on her knees, untouched. I saw her tears falling to the plate. Her twins sat beside her eating, unconcerned. No-one could console her, and soon they forgot to even try."

"That's the pork's fault," I said. "Too delicious."

"Don't be cruel. Sometimes I wonder if I'm really still living with Ismael Pasos, or with a stranger, a monster. It's better to think that everyone was suffering like I was, Ismael, and was saddened. No-one asked for another drink. There was no music, just as Father Albornoz would have liked. They ate and they left."

"I'm not cruel. I repeat that it hurts me that any man should be held captive against his will, no matter what he has, or what he doesn't have, because they're taking those who have nothing too; that said, it's better to disappear voluntarily, on one's own, so they don't disappear us by force, which must be much worse. I'm grateful for my age, half a step from the grave, and I feel sorry for the children, who have a hard road ahead of them, with all this death they're inheriting, and through no fault of their own. But compared to Marcos Saldarriaga's fate I'm much more distressed by that of Carmina Lucero, the baker. They took her too, the same day."

"Carmina," my wife screamed.

"I found out today."

"No-one ever told us."

"They only talked about Marcos Saldarriaga."

"Carmina," my wife said again. And I saw she was starting to cry. Why did I tell her?

"Who told you?" she asked me with a sob.

"Lie down first," I answered.

But she stayed there, aghast.

"Who was it?" she said.

"Maestro Claudino. He fixed my knee today. I have to take him a hen."

"A hen," she said, without understanding. Then she added, strangely, because we have two hens, while she turned out the light and lay down beside me, "And how will you buy it?"

Not waiting for my answer, she began to speak of Carmina Lucero: she had never known such a good woman, and she thought of Carmina's husband and her children, how they must have suffered.

She said, "When things at home weren't going well, Carmina gave us as much bread as we needed on credit."

Every once in a while I would hear her moan fade into the hot air we were breathing, just when I thought that restorative sleep was at last about to come and help us, and indeed we were more than exhausted resting on a bed in a town in a country under torture and I did not yet dare to reveal that Carmina had already died in captivity two years ago; nevertheless: that night neither of us could sleep.

Why stay in bed? Dawn breaks and I leave the house: I retrace my steps back towards the cliff. On the mountain across the way, at this time of the morning, the scattered houses look eternal, far from each other, but united anyway because they are and always will be on the same mountain, high and blue. Years ago, before Otilia, I imagined myself living in one of them for the rest of my life. No-one lives in them today, or very few of them anyway; not more than two years ago there were close to ninety families, and what with the war – the drug traffickers and army, guerrillas and para-militaries – there are only sixteen left. Many died, most of them must have had to leave: who knows how many families are going to stay on now? Will we stay? I look away from the landscape because for the first time I cannot stand it, everything has changed now –

but not the way it should have, damn it.

A pig walks towards me along the edge of the cliff, sniffing the ground. It stops for a moment at my feet, lifts its snout, snorts, eyes up my shoes: whose pig is this? All through the town, every once in a while, a pig or a hen will wander, no sign of an owner. It is possible that it is I who has forgotten the names of the owners of the pigs; I used to recognize them. And what if I took this pig to Maestro Claudino, instead of a hen?

I hear a shout in the early morning, and then a shot. It is up ahead, at the corner. The detonation has formed a black cloud of smoke there. A white shadow runs across the street, from that corner to the next. Nothing more is heard, except footsteps hurrying away till they disappear. Today I got up early to go out, better to go out, one cannot go for a quiet stroll these days; I hear my footsteps now, echoing one behind the other, speeding up, in a definite direction; what am I doing here, at five in the morning? I discover that the route back to my house is the same one the running shadow took. I stop, it is not prudent to follow fleeing shadows, there are no more shots to be heard, a private matter? Could be: it does not seem like the war, it is *another* war: someone caught someone stealing, someone simply caught someone, who? I keep walking, stop, listen: nothing else, no-one else. My knee: "You have to rest it for three days," Maestro Claudino warned me, and here I am back and forth. Will you start hurting me again, knee? No, my painless steps go round the corners, I am cured, what an embarrassment that pain was, Otilia, what a premonition, what a mistake, let no-one miss me when I'm gone, but let no-one have to help me to the toilet, Otilia, die after I do.

I walk without knowing where to, in the opposite direction from the shadow, away from the gunshot; better find a place where I can sit and watch the sun rise over San José, although I could use another shot of cane liquor for this other pain as if inside my breath, what is it? Can it be that I am going to die? More shots ring out, machine-gun bursts this time – I freeze, they are distant – so it wasn't *another* war, it *is* the real war, we are going mad, or we have gone mad, where have I finished up? It's the school: habit brought me here.

"*Profesor*, you're up early to teach?"

It's Fanny, who was Fanny? The caretaker. Smaller than she used to be, the same apron as years ago. Did I not slip into her camp bed more than many years ago, did I not smell her? Yes. She smelled of sugar-water. And her head has been painted white. She still lives here, but now none of her children are with her, what am I saying, her children must be old by now, they will have gone. I remember her husband: he died young, on his way back from some saint's day fiesta; he fell into a ditch and his mule landed on top of him.

"*Profesor*, it seems they took someone today or yesterday."

Her eyes are as bright as ever, like the time I smelled her, but her body is in ruins worse than mine.

And she says: "You had better go home."

"That's where I'm going."

And she closes the door, just like that: she won't remember what I remember. I set off again towards home, on the other side of the town. I am far away; when did I leave, at what time? I simply did not want to follow the direction of the running shadow. Now I can go back, the shadow will have gone now, I think, and I think I'm going back but in the plaza the soldiers stop me, they escort me, at gunpoint, to a group of men sitting on the steps of the church. We know each other; over there I see Celmiro, older than I am: a friend dozing. Some say good morning. Arrested. Today Otilia will not be bored by my news. I watch the brightening dawn, which descends from the mountaintop like fluttering sheets; the weather is still cool, but it makes way, minute by minute, for the stubborn heat, if I had an orange in my hand, if the shade of the orange tree, if Otilia was looking over her fish, if the cats.

A soldier asks for our identification cards, another verifies the numbers on the screen of a portable machine. Those who were sleeping in San José begin to come out of their houses. They know very well that we are the unfortunate ones who got up early. It is our turn. We the early risers are interrogated: why did you get up early today, what were you doing in the street? Only some can go, more or less half of us: a soldier reads a list of names.

"These can go," he said, and I was astonished: I did not hear my name.

Anyway I leave with those who are leaving. A sort of anger, indifference, helps me walk through the rifles without drawing attention to myself. In fact, they do not even look at me.

Old Celmiro, older than me, a friend, follows my example: he was not named either, and this mortifies him.

"What's wrong with these people?" he says to me. "What could they have to accuse us of? Fuck all." He complains that none of his sons came to get him when they found out.

And we hear the protests of Rodrigo Pinto, young and worried; weakly he protests; he crumples his white hat in his hands; he is from the next district, lives in the mountains, relatively far from our town, but nevertheless he is arrested and will stay arrested for who knows how long; they will not allow him to go to his house, which is on the front line, halfway up the next mountain; he tells us his wife is pregnant, his four children alone and waiting for him; he came into town to buy oil and sugarloaf, but he dares not follow my example and that of Celmiro: he is not old enough to cross the line unnoticed.

It has been three or four long hours staring at each other, more resigned than outraged. It goes on all the time, when something happens and one gets up earlier than usual. They load the ones left up into an army truck; they are probably going to interrogate them more closely at the base.

"Someone was taken," people are saying. "Who did they take this time?"

Nobody knows, and nobody is in a hurry to find out either; someone being taken is a commonplace occurrence, but it is a sensitive subject to enquire about too much, to be excessively concerned; some women, while we were being held, came to speak to their husbands. Otilia did not come; she will still be sleeping, she will dream that I am asleep at her side, and now it is noon, hard to believe; where had the time gone? But gone it had, as usual, as ever.

*

"So, *profesor*? You're a light sleeper too."

"I didn't know you were with me," I answer.

"I wasn't. I was just watching. I didn't want to disturb you, *profesor*, not to bother you. You looked as though you were dreaming of angels."

And Dr Gentil Orduz comes over to me, opening his arms, his square-rimmed glasses, his white shirt flashing in the sun.

"I was not detained," he informs me. "But you're so amusing, it was funny to watch you, *profesor*, why didn't you resist? Tell them I am *Profesor* Pasos, and that's that, they'd let you go immediately."

"Those boys don't know me."

I confront the satisfied, pink, healthy face that is too close to me. He pats me on the shoulders.

"Have you heard?" he says. "They took the Brazilian."

"The Brazilian," I repeat.

No wonder he did not appear at Hortensia Galindo's; Otilia did not mention him; was that not his horse I saw alone, saddled up, trotting casually in the night, on my way back from Maestro Claudino's.

"You could see it coming, couldn't you?" Dr Orduz asks me. "Let's have a beer, *profesor*. My treat: a man feels good in your company, why is that?"

We make ourselves comfortable in the aisle that looks on to the street. "Again at Chepe's shop," I say to myself. "It's fate." Chepe greets us from the table opposite, with his wife, who is pregnant. They are both having chicken soup. What wouldn't I give for some broth instead of a beer. Chepe exudes cheerfulness, energy. After all, his first child, his heir, is on its way. A few years ago they kidnapped Chepe, but he was able to escape quite soon: he threw himself over a cliff, hid in a hole in the mountain, for six days: he tells the story with pride, laughing, as if it is a joke. Life in San José is resuming its course, it appears. Today it is not Chepe, but a young girl, who waits on us; a white daisy shines in her black hair. Who told me all the girls had left town?

"It must be your age," the doctor answers himself, "that makes one feel so at peace at your side."

"My age?" I am amazed. "Old age does not bring peace."

"But there is peace in wisdom, isn't there, *profesor*? You are a venerable old man. The Brazilian was telling me about you."

I wonder if he is saying this with a double meaning.

"As far as I know," I say, "he is not Brazilian. He is from here, as Colombian as we are, from Quindío. Why is he called the Brazilian?"

"That, *profesor*, neither you nor I can know. Might as well ask why they took him."

Dr Orduz must be getting on for forty, a good age. He has been the director of the hospital for six years or so. Single, with good reason, he has two nurses and a very young lady doctor doing her rural training year under his charge. He is the famous surgeon in these parts. He carried out a delicate heart operation on an Indian in the middle of the jungle, at night, successfully, and all on his own, with no anaesthetic, no instruments. He has been lucky: both times the guerrillas wanted to take him he was far away from San José, in El Palo. And the one time the paramilitaries came looking for him he managed to hide in a corner of the market, burrowing all the way into a sack of corn cobs. They do not want to take Dr Orduz to ask for a ransom, they say, but to use him for what he is, a great surgeon.

He seems settled in San José.

"At first I was shocked to see so much blood spilled," he tends to say, "but now I'm used to it."

Dr Orduz laughs all the time, even more than Chepe. Though not from around here, he has not wanted to leave, like other doctors have.

His voice subsides, becomes a whisper.

"I understand," he says, "that the Brazilian paid his protection money, to the paras as well as the guerrillas, on the sly, in the hope that they'd leave him be, you know? So, why did they take him? Who knows. He was a cautious fellow, and he was about to pack up and leave. He didn't manage to. They tell me they found all the cattle on his ranch with their throats slit. He must have annoyed someone, but who?"

He spread his arms in a wide shrug at the moment the girl brought us the beer.

"Doctor," Chepe shouts from his table. His wife looks up at the ceiling, blushing and anxious.

Orduz looks over at them with his grey eyes.

"We have finally decided," Chepe goes on. "We want to know if it'll be a boy or a girl."

"Right away," Orduz replies, but does not stand up. He just pushes his chair back and takes off his glasses. "Let's see, Carmenza, show me that belly. From there, like that, in profile."

She sighs. And she also pushes back her chair and obediently lifts up her blouse, up to where her breasts begin. It is a seven- or eight-month belly, white, which shines more in the light. The doctor stares long and hard.

"More in profile," he says, and squints.

"Like this?" She moves to one side. Her nipples are large and dark, and her breasts much bigger, full.

"A girl," says the doctor, and puts his glasses back on.

The waitress who served our beers squeals, then giggles, and runs back inside the shop.

Chepe's wife drops her blouse. She has suddenly turned serious.

"Then she'll be called Angélica," she says.

"O.K." Chepe laughs, claps once and rubs his hands together, leaning over his bowl.

The troop of soldiers was marching down the street. One of those boys stopped in front of our table, on the other side of the wooden railing, and told us furiously that we could not drink, that prohibition was in effect.

"Oh, we can drink," said the doctor, "but you won't let us. Calm down, it's just a beer, I already asked Captain Berrío. I am Dr Orduz, don't you recognize me?"

The soldier goes away reluctantly among the green blotch of the rest of the boys on their way out of town, in formation, slowly, with the slowness of those who know they could well be going to their deaths. To run forward they would need a shout from Captain Berrío behind them. But Berrío is nowhere to be seen. They are very few, and very distinct, the combatants who run of their own volition towards death. I think they no longer exist; only in history.

"I bet today one of those devils is going to kill me," a boy said to me one day.

He had stopped in my doorway, asked for water.

They were leaving to confront an advance. Fear was twisting him, he was green with panic: with every reason, because he was young.

I am going to die, he said, and they did kill him: I saw his rigid face when they brought him back; and not just him, there were quite a few more.

Where are these boys going now? They will try to liberate a stranger. Soon the town will be left without soldiers, for a time. I watch the street, while the doctor across from me talks. The girls who have not gone away, because they cannot, because their families do not have the wherewithal or they do not know how or to whom to send them, are the prettiest, I think, because they are the ones who stay, the last ones. A group of them run away in the opposite direction from where the troop is heading. I see their skirts flying, I hear their frightened cries, but also, among them, other cries, the excitement of a farewell to the soldiers.

"A single battalion, in San José, against two armies," the doctor says. And he observes me looking sad, perhaps wondering whether I am listening to him. I listen, now: "We are more helpless than this cockroach," he says, and crushes an enormous cockroach under his heel. "The Mayor was right to ask for more troops."

And I stare at the smudge of cockroach, a meagre little relief map.

"Well," I say, "cockroaches will survive the end of the world."

"If they're extraterrestrials," he says, and guffaws, without conviction. And he stares at me the harder. He has, in any case, a wide, permanent smile on his face. Now he bangs the table: "Did you not hear the Mayor on the radio? It was broadcast on television as well, and he told the truth, he said that San José has only one battalion of infantry and a police post, and that it amounts to the same as nothing, being in the hands of the bandits; he said that if the Minister of Defence can come here, he should come, so that he can take stock of the situation himself. He needed balls to say that; he could be removed from his post, for shooting his mouth off."

How will sweet Geraldina be doing? Otilia will surely be keeping her company. Warm water wets my leg. My problem, once in a while, is that I forget to go to the lavatory. I should have consulted Maestro Claudino about that. And that is how it is: I look at myself: my trousers are a little wet between the legs, it was not the fear, was it, Ismael, or was it? It was not the bursts of gunfire, the shadow that fled. No. Just old age.

"Are you listening to me, *profesor*?"

"My knee hurts," I lied.

"Come to the hospital on Monday, and we'll have

a look. Now I have other things to see to. Which knee? The left one? Well, we can tell from which way you limp."

I say goodbye. I want to hear, want to see Geraldina, find out what is happening with her.

The doctor stands up too.

"I'm going where you're going," he tells me mischievously, "to your neighbour's. I gave her a tranquillizer a few hours ago. She was hysterical. We'll see if she's asleep yet," and, again, he pats me on the shoulders, on the back.

They trouble me: his two hot hands feel dreadful in this heat, his two soft, delicate surgeon's hands, the fingers burning, accustomed to so much death, pressing the sweat of my shirt against my skin.

"Don't touch me," I say. "Don't touch me today, please."

The doctor laughs again and walks along beside me:

"I understand, *profesor*. Being arrested just for getting up early would put anyone in a rotten mood, isn't that so?"

The empanada seller still persists from the same distant corner: we hear his shout to no-one in particular, his violent plea, *Heeeey*, the same as ever for years now, looking for customers where there are none – where there cannot be any, now. He is not the same chubby boy who arrived in San José with his little stove on wheels, the roving firebox he lights with petrol, spreading blue flames beneath the big fryer. He must be close to thirty now: his head is shaved; he has a lazy eye; a deep scar marks his narrow forehead; his ears are tiny, unreal. Nobody knows his name, everyone calls him "Hey". He arrived in San José knowing no-one, turned to stone behind his stove, the enormous noisy crate where the oil bubbles, folded his arms, and there began to sell and continues to sell the same empanadas that he prepares himself, and repeats to anyone his story, which is the same, but so ferocious that it does not make one want to go back to eat more empanadas: he shows the metal draining rack, points to the fryer full of black oil, sinks the draining rack into it and then holds up the rack: he says at that temperature its edge could slice a throat as easily as cutting through butter, and he says that he himself had to use it on an empanada thief in Bogotá: "One who had the bright idea to steal from me, that was pure self-defence," and while he says it he waves the draining rack a little, a sword in your head, and shouts to no one, at the top of his voice, deafening you: *Heeeey!*

I did not return for his empanadas, and I do not suppose the doctor did either. It seems we were both thinking the same thing.

"He's a murderer in his dreams," Orduz says, looking away from the empanada vendor with a slight revulsion.

We carry on down the empty, dusty street.

"Or he's terrified," I say. "Who knows?"

"He's the strangest fellow I've ever met, I'm sure he sells his empanadas, he's got money, but in all these years I've never seen him with a woman, never even with a dog. I always see him watching the news, at Chepe's, stuck to the door, leaning against it, more absorbed than at the cinema; two years ago, when they filmed the streets of this town of peace, when the

73

church had just been blown up, and it was our turn to see ourselves on the television news for the first time, surrounded by dead bodies, they showed him for a second, in the background, and he recognized himself on his corner, pointed at himself and shouted *Heeeey* so loud he almost broke the windows, our eardrums and hearts.

"And then he went pale when he heard Chepe shout: 'Go and shout at your corner.'

"And he, with another louder shout: 'Hasn't a body got a right to shout?' and left.

"They tell me he sleeps rough, behind the church."

As if responding to his words, we hear the distant *Heeeey*, to which we are all accustomed in San José. The doctor turns to me, astonished, and seems to want my opinion. I did not say anything because we had almost arrived at the Brazilian's house, and I did not want to converse any more.

We saw Captain Berrío's jeep parked in front of the door.

"Berrío hasn't gone out to look for the Brazilian yet," Orduz says, with inordinate surprise.

And then we arrived at the large metal gate, which was open, as Mauricio Rey was coming out, all dressed up in white.

"It looks as though the last men left in this town

are enjoying offering their condolences for the newly departed," Orduz manages to say to me.

I know Mauricio Rey is not to his liking, and vice versa.

And still I hear the doctor continue indecently: "Anyone would think that Rey is no longer drunk. Look how straight he walks. He knows how."

"Isn't it true, *profesor*, that walking with doctors makes one ill? You'll catch a cold at the very least," Mauricio says to me and the doctor laughs politely: just as well we are talking in front of Geraldina's house.

We look at each other as if in consultation.

"Berrío is still collecting information," Rey says. "I think he's scared to go after them."

"As usual," the doctor says.

"But go on in, gentlemen," Rey encourages us, "and comfort Geraldina: they didn't just take the Brazilian, but the children as well."

"The children?" I say.

"The children," Rey says, and makes way for us.

For the first time I do not think of Geraldina but of the children. I see them tumbling in the garden, I hear them. I cannot believe it. Dr Orduz goes inside first. I start to catch up with him when Rey takes my arm and pulls me to one side. He is actually still drunk, I discover from his breath, from his reddened eyes that clash with his white suit. He has shaved, and the drunker he is the younger he looks, preserved in alcohol, they say, although he stopped playing chess because he started falling asleep between moves.

Now I see him stagger for an instant, but he recovers.

"A drink?" he laughs.

"This is not the time," I say.

And he, breathing his stink in my face, completely distracted, his eyes floating along the empty street, amazed at himself.

"Be careful, *profesor*, the world is full of sober people." He shakes my hand vigorously and moves away.

"Where are you going, Mauricio?" I ask. "You should lie down. This is no day to be out on the town."

"Out on the town? I'm just going to the plaza for a minute, to find out what's going on."

We are interrupted by the Captain's departure, in the company of two soldiers. The three of them clamber into the jeep. Berrío greets us with a nod of his fat, pink head; he goes right past us without a word.

"Didn't I tell you?" Mauricio Rey shouts to me from the distance.

I had never been here, in the small living room of the Brazilian's house. Cool and quiet, decorated with flowers, wicker chairs and lots of cushions around, inviting sleep, I say to myself, standing in the doorway, hearing what people are saying, but most of all absorbing the intimate air of Geraldina's house, which is her smell, her own smell of home. I hear the doctor, then a sob, the voices of several women, a distant cough. I discover first of all that Otilia is not in the living room. I go in and say hello to the neighbours.

Professor Lesmes, the school's headmaster for a few months now, approaches me, takes me to one side, as if I were his property, with faith in me as a fellow teacher, knowing that I had been in charge of the school.

"Lamentable," he says, not realizing that he is preventing me from speaking to Geraldina. "I came to San José to do nothing," he exclaims in a whisper. "Not a single child attends, and how could they? A barricade has been put up in front of the school; if there is a skirmish it won't be long before we suffer the consequences, we'll be the first."

"Excuse me," I say, and look at Geraldina.

"I've only just heard," I say in greeting. "I'm so sorry, Geraldina. If there's anything we can do, we're here to help."

"Thank you, sir," she says.

Her eyes are swollen from crying, this is another Geraldina, and, just like Hortensia Galindo, she has dressed all in black, but still (I think, unable to stop myself), there still, rounder and more resplendent, are her knees. She holds her chin quite high, as if offering her neck to an invisible someone or something – to a deadly face, or a weapon – her brow furrowed, completely defeated; her pupils shine with fever, she entwines and untwines her fingers.

"Sir," she says, "Otilia was asking for you. She seemed very worried."

"I'm going to go and find her now."

But I stay where I am, and she keeps looking at me.

"Did you hear, *profesor*?" she sobs. "My son, my children, they took them, it's unforgivable."

Dr Orduz takes her pulse, says the usual things to her: calm down, a strong and serene Geraldina is more help to everyone.

"But do you know what this is like?" she asks him, with sudden force, as if rebelling.

"I know, we all know," the doctor replies, looking around.

We all, in our turn, look at each other, and it is as if we did not really know, as if in a surreptitious way we understood, without shame, that we do not know what this is like, but this not knowing is not our fault, this we do seem to know.

She has turned back to me.

"He came in at midnight with other men and took the children, just like that, *profesor*. He took the children, saying nothing, without a word to me, like a dead man. The other men held guns on him; I'm sure they had forbidden him to speak, don't you think? That's why he could not say anything to me. I don't want to think he couldn't speak out of pure cowardice. He himself took the children by the hand.

"To suffer more, I have only to remember the children asking: 'Where are you taking us? Why did you wake us up?'

"'Come on, let's go,' he said. 'It's just a little walk,' he told them, not a word to me, as if I was not the mother of my son.

"They went and they left me, they said I would have to take care of arranging the payment. That they would be in touch, they said, and they dared to laugh as they told me that. They took them, *profesor*, who knows for how long, oh God, just when we were about to leave, not only this town, but this damned country."

The doctor offers her a sedative, someone brings a glass of water. She ignores the pill, the water. Her sleepless eyes look at me unseeing.

"Then I couldn't move," she says. "I stayed still until dawn. I heard you go out, I heard your door, but I could not manage to scream. By the time I was able to walk the sun was already up, it was the first day of my life without my son. Then I wished the earth would swallow me up, do you understand?"

Again the doctor offers her the pill, the water, and she obeys without taking her eyes from mine, and she has her unseeing eyes fixed on me still as I walk to the door.

I do not find Otilia at home. I am in the garden, which is unchanged, as if nothing had happened, although everything has happened: I see the ladder there, leaning against the wall; in the fountain the flashing orange fish swim; one of the cats stretching in the sun looks at me, makes me think of Geraldina's eyes, Geraldina dressed in black overnight.

"*Profesor*," a voice shouts from the door, which I have left open.

In the doorway waits Sultana, with her daughter, the girl who was looking after Mauricio Rey on his sick day. As if Rey had sent her to me. But it is nothing to do with Mauricio Rey: it is my own wife, I find out, who has arranged with Sultana for her daughter to come and help once a week in the orchard.

"We met your wife at the corner," Sultana explains.

"She told me she was going to ask about you at the presbytery. You'll have to go and find her: this is no day to be wandering the streets."

I listen to Sultana, but I see only the girl: she no longer has messy hair, or the same look in her eyes; now she is just an impatient child, or maybe bored at the thought of work.

"It won't be much," I encourage her. "You just have to finish picking the oranges and then you can go home."

Otilia has brought me temptation in person, and she does not even know it. The girl is wearing a simple dress and goes barefoot, but she does not shine now, she drifts down the corridor in little hops, peeks through the kitchen door, timidly looks at the two bedrooms, the living room, she fidgets, vulnerable and scrawny, like a little bird. She does not look like her mother: Sultana is large, big-boned, strong; she is wearing her eternal, incandescent red baseball cap; her prominent belly does not diminish her strength: she cleans the church, the police station, the town hall all on her own, washes and irons clothes, makes her living that way and wants her daughter to do the same.

"See that, Cristina?" she asks. "You'll come here once a week, it's easy to find."

They carry on out into the garden. The agitation, the shock of seeing this girl walking, of pursuing and perusing this girl, perceiving the fatality of the wild aroma, raw but sharp, that each of her steps gives off, makes you forget what is most important to you in the world, Ismael. I shall speak to her, sooner or later I shall make her laugh, tell her a tale and, while she is up the ladder, I shall surely pick flowers nearby.

"I've never seen your garden," Sultana says. "You've got fish, you like flowers, *profesor*. You or your wife?"

"Both of us."

"I have to go," she suddenly shouts to the sky, says goodbye to her daughter with a wave: "I'll come back for you, don't go anywhere, stay right here," and she shakes my hand with a man's strength, and leaves the house.

Cristina stands looking at me in the middle of a shaft of sunshine fragmented from passing through the branches of the orange tree. She blinks. She runs a shining hand over an even shinier face: does she remember me?

"I'm so thirsty," she says.

"Go to the kitchen. Make some lemonade, there's ice."

"Ice." As if pronouncing a supernatural word she runs past me, leaving me plunged in the blend of her breeze, am I staggering? I stretch out in the rocking chair, at the edge of the sun, and stay there, hearing the distant kitchen noise, the fridge door that opens, closes, the glasses and the ice clinking, the force with which

Cristina pushes and strains with the lemons, wringing them out. Then nothing is heard: how much time has gone by? I grow tired of looking at my knees, my shoes; I raise my eyes: a blurry bird flies soundlessly between the trees. It is the afternoon silence, which increases in the garden, becomes hardened, remote, as if it were night-time and the whole world asleep. The atmosphere, from one moment to the next, is unbreathable; it might rain at dusk; a slow feeling of unease overtakes everything, not just human, but plants, the cats who watch from nearby, the unmoving fish; it is as though one were not inside one's own house, in spite of so being, as if we found ourselves in the middle of the street, in the sight of all weapons, defenceless, with no wall to protect your body and your soul, what is going on? What is happening to me? Is it that I am going to die?

When the girl comes back with the glasses of lemonade, keen to drink her own, I no longer recognize her: who is this young girl who looks at me, who talks to me? Never in my life have I forgotten like this, out of the blue, worse than a slap in the face. It is as if, in all this time, a cloth of fog had fallen on top of the sun, darkening everything: that is why I suddenly felt an enormous fear that Otilia is alone, today, walking through these peaceful streets where it is possible the war will come again. Let it come, let it return, I say to myself, shout to myself, but not with my Otilia without me.

"Smithereens," I say aloud, and stand up to leave.

"Aren't you going to have some lemonade?"

"You have mine," I tell the girl, recognizing her at last, and, lost, I ask her, "Where did Sultana tell me Otilia was going?"

She looks at me perplexed, not understanding.

But eventually: "To the presbytery."

Why would you think, Otilia, that I am at the presbytery? It has been years since I have gone to see the priest.

My arms and legs swing with no rhythm whatsoever as I proceed along the streets as if through hanks of cotton, what bad dream are these empty, uneasy streets; down each of them I am pursued by physical, floating, dark air, although I see that the sun weighs heavily on the streets: why did I not bring my hat? To think that not long ago I prided myself on my memory, one of these days I am going to forget myself, I shall leave me forgotten in some corner of the house, forget to take myself out for a walk, the neighbours are doing the right thing – I say, I repeat – there are fewer and fewer people in the town, and with reason, anything could happen, everything could happen, and whatever happens there will be war, screams will echo, powder will explode, I only stop saying it when I discover that I am talking out loud as I walk, to whom, to whom?

Only in the plaza are there scattered groups of men; their voices can be heard and occasionally a whistle, as if it were a Sunday. I make for the door of the presbytery, just past the entrance to the church itself, but before touching the knocker I turn back: in the plaza the same dispersed groups, apparently calm, habitual, turn to inspect me briefly: seeing them really is as if they were all flooded in fog, the same fog I saw in the garden; is it that I am going to die today? A silence identical to the fog encloses our faces, from all sides. It is possible that shots will be heard, from here, or that they will reach our very ears, graze them. Then it will be time to flee. I knock with haste. Señora Blanca opens the door. Her nervous, powdered face peeks out around the edge of the door. She is Father Albornoz's assistant, his sacristan, his right hand, the one who collects money during mass and probably counts it, while Father Albornoz rests, soaking his feet in a pail of salted water, as I saw him do on every one of my visits.

"Your wife has just left," says the woman. "She was here, asking for you."

"I am playing cat and mouse with Otilia," I tell her. I am about to say goodbye, but she interrupts me.

"The Father wants to see you." And she opens the door all the way.

I see the priest, at the back, his aquiline profile, in his black habit, his black schoolboy shoes, Bible in hand: the churchyard cherimoya and lemon trees form a backdrop to his grey head, the cool garden, beautified by large azalea bushes and clumps of geraniums.

"Father Albornoz, I am looking for my wife."

"Come in, come in, *profesor*, just for a coffee."

He was another of my pupils, from the age of eight. I was a boy as well: I was only twenty-two years old when I returned to San José to the teacher's post, and began to teach for the first time in my life, getting used to the idea that it would be for three years at most in my home town, out of gratitude, and then I would go, where? I never knew, and in any case I never went, because here I would end up, almost buried. Something similar happened to Horacio Albornoz: he left and came back as a priest. He came to pay his respects the first day.

He still remembered the poem by Pombo that he and his classmates memorized for me: *And this magnificent carpet / Oh Earth! Who to you gave it? / And the trees to cool and shade it? / And the Earth says: God did.*

"I'm sure my vocation springs from there," he told me, laughing.

And we began to visit each other once a week: we would drink coffee at my house or in the presbytery, we talked about the news in the paper, the Pope's latest dictates, and once in a while a confidence or two would slip out, until we reached that rare state of mind that allows us to believe there is another friend in the world.

A few months after Albornoz came back as a priest, a woman arrived in San José with a baby girl in her arms; she got down from the dusty bus – the only passenger – and went directly to the presbytery, in search of help and work. Father Albornoz, who up till then had refused the sporadic offers from several ladies of good will to take charge of his cleaning, his cooking and making his bed, of his clothes and his meagre things, immediately accepted the stranger into the parish. She is now Señora Blanca, who over the years has become the sacristan. Her daughter is now one of the many girls who left, years ago; and Señora Blanca goes on being just a shadow, silently kind, so delicate she seems invisible.

One afternoon years ago, when instead of having coffee we were drinking wine, three bottles of Spanish wine that the Bishop of Neiva had given him, Father Albornoz asked the sacristan to leave us alone. He was sad in spite of the wine, his eyes were watery, his mouth downcast: I even thought he might burst into tears.

"And if not you, who can I tell?" he said at last.

"Me." I said.

"Or the Pope," he answered, "if I were brave enough."

Such an opening worried me. The priest was a grimace of repentance. He spent a long minute screwing up his courage to begin before allowing me to gather, through puerile allusions, and without neglecting the wine, that Señora Blanca was also his woman, and that the girl was the daughter of them both, that they slept in the same bed like any married couple every night in this peaceable town. I know very well that savage gossip did the rounds from the start, when the woman and child arrived after him, but it occurred to none of us to be scandalized. What for?

"And what does it matter?" I told him. "Was that not a healthy and sane attitude, so different to the ones adopted by so many other priests in so many countries, hypocrisy, bitterness, even perversion, abuse, rape of children? Did he not go on being, most importantly, the parish priest?"

"Yes," he replied in confusion, his eyes attentive, as if it had never occurred to him. But he added: "It is not easy to overcome. One suffers, before and after."

After another minute he decided: "What I am never going to give up is the Lord's work, my mission, in the midst of the daily sadness of this country."

And it seemed that, at last, in this way, he had found the absolution that he needed. I still wanted to tell him, excusing him: "You are certainly not the first, this is very common in many towns," but I began to speak of other things: now he seemed to have tremendous regret at having confided his secret to me, and perhaps desired that I would soon leave, and soon forget it, but I shall never forget the shadow of Señora Blanca, that afternoon, when she saw me to the door, the wide mute smile on her face, so grateful she seemed to be about to kiss me.

There I left them years ago, here I find them.

There I left them because Father Albornoz never asked me to visit again, and nor did he visit me. Here I find them, the same but older, while we sit in the small reception room of the presbytery, with the frosted window overlooking the plaza. After the attack two years ago, Father Albornoz travelled to Bogotá and persuaded the government to pay for the resurrection of the dynamited church: allowing the church to remain destroyed would be a victory for the destroyers, whoever they were, he argued; so another church rose in the same place, a better house for God and for the Father, said Dr Orduz, who unlike the priest did not obtain any aid for his hospital.

If the priest is going to talk to me in front of

Señora Blanca, it is not possible, I think, that Otilia has confided in him about my wall and my ladder, my secret. Otilia: you would not be able to undergo my confession in my place. So, what is he going to say? We drink our coffee without a word. On the other side of the frosted window one can make out the whole plaza, the tall oaks that surround it, the imposing town hall. The plaza is a sort of sloping rectangle; we, in the presbytery, are up above; the town hall is down below.

"And if it happens again?" the Father asks me, if the guerrillas get as far as this plaza, as before?"

"I don't think so," I tell him. "I don't think they will this time."

We hear some screams, from the plaza. Señora Blanca does not flinch; she sips her coffee as if she were in heaven.

"I only wanted to tell you, Ismael, to come back and see me, and soon. Come back as a friend, or as a penitent, whenever you want; don't forget me, what's wrong with you? If I don't visit you it's because of what happened today, what's happened since yesterday, and what will happen tomorrow, unfortunately for this town in torment. We no longer have the right to have friends. We must struggle and pray even in our dreams. But the doors of the church are open to all, my duty is to receive the lamb who has gone astray."

His sacristan watches him transfixed. As for me, it seems that Otilia did confess on my behalf.

"These are difficult days for everyone," the priest goes on. "Uncertainty reigns even in the heart, and that is when we must put to the test our faith in God, who sooner or later will redeem us entirely."

I stand up.

"Thank you, Father, for the coffee. I have to go and find Otilia. You know better than anyone that this is no day to be wandering the streets looking for each other."

"She came here specifically, asking after you, and we talked. That reminded me of how long it has been since we've seen each other, Ismael. Don't be such a recluse."

He sees me to the door, but there we stop, immersed in an unexpected, whispered conversation: so many things have happened that we have not discussed – because of absence – that we try to go over everything, in one minute, and so we recall, in still quieter voices, Father Ortiz, from El Tablón, whom we knew, who was killed, after being tortured, by paramilitaries: they burned his testicles, chopped off his ears, and then they shot him for promulgating liberation theology.

"What can one say, then, when it comes to the sermon?" the Father asks me, his hands open, eyes wide. "Anyone can accuse us of whatever they like, merely for appealing for peace, appealing to God," and, with that, as if he decided on it at the last moment, like someone making up their mind to take a short stroll, he leaves the presbytery with me, tells the sacristan to lock the door, to wait for him. "I'll only be a minute," he says, as she stares at him in terror.

We start down the steps of the presbytery, in watchful silence; what have we not revealed? From the middle of the plaza a slow group of men come up to say hello, and the Father stops; he wants to carry on the conversation with me, but the arrival of his parishioners will prevent it; he shrugs, makes a vague gesture and carries on down the slope beside me; he attends to the men with a comforting smile, without a word; he listens to them all with equal interest; some are from this town, others from the mountains: it is not advisable to stay in the mountains when confrontations draw near; they have already hidden their children in friends' houses; they have come to find out what awaits us; neither the Mayor nor his spokesman is in the town hall; there is no-one in the offices of the municipal council; where are they? What are we going to do? How long will it last?

The uncertainty is the same for everyone; Father Albornoz replies, spreading his arms; what can he know? He speaks to them as in his sermons, and maybe he is right, putting oneself in his place: the fear of being misinterpreted, of ending up accused by this or that army, of annoying a drugs trafficker – who can count on a spy among the very parishioners who surround him – has turned him into a concerto of faltering words, where everything converges in faith: pray to heaven in the hope that this fratricidal war does not reach San José again, may reason prevail, may Eusebio Almida be returned, another innocent sacrificed, yet another, Monseñor Rubiano has warned us that kidnapping is a diabolical reality, faith in our creator, he exhorts us, and raises his index finger, after darkness comes the light, and, something truly absurd, which no-one understands straight away, but everyone listens to and accepts because there must be a reason for the Father to say it, he announces that the Divine Child has been named this morning as the national religious figure, that our country remains consecrated to the Christ Child, we must pray, he insists, but in fact he does not say a prayer and no-one seems prepared to go along with the idea.

Mauricio Rey is also among those who approach. He tells me – for a change – that my wife is looking for me.

"She asked me if I'd seen you," he says. "I told her I'd just seen you at the Brazilian's house. That's where she went."

As I am about to take my leave I see, diagonally opposite us, down below, the first soldiers appear, in flight; everyone else has seen them too and falls silent, waiting: every gaze converges on that point. The soldiers do not seem to have arrived in an orderly fashion, as they had left, but rather it seems as if they are being chased; they take cover in different places, ducking down at the same corner they have just arrived at, taking aim.

Now I see, around me, faces suddenly unknown – although they belong to people I know – exchanging horrified looks, crowding together unawares; there is a faint clamour that seems to arise from deep down in their chests.

Someone mutters: *Shit, they're back.*

The soldiers stay alert and still; there must be twelve or fifteen of them; none have turned to look at us, to recommend anything, as on other occasions; at that moment we hear bursts of gunfire, explosions, but still outside of town. A murmur of cold admiration runs up our spines – loud now, full – these shadows I see around me, the same or worse than me, engulf me in a whirl of voices and faces distorted by fear; I see in a flash the silhouette of Father Albornoz fleeing to his presbytery, as fast as a deer; an ambulance appears at the same corner, holes all along its flank, but moving at a good speed, and disappears in the direction of the hospital behind a dust cloud; other soldiers have made their entrance at the top corner, and they shout to those below, in haste; the shots, the explosions, intensify, close by, and still no-one knows for certain what part of town they are coming from, where to run to? All of a sudden they stop and are replaced by a silence like breathing; the combatants take up their positions, and we, where to go?

At that moment the Captain's jeep drives up noisily, bouncing over the stones of the plaza: Berrío leaps out of it and looks at our group, will perhaps order us to go home, to anywhere under cover; he is pale, dishevelled, he opens his mouth, but without a sound, as if swallowing air; several seconds pass like that.

"Guerrillas," he shouts all of a sudden, pointing at us, "you are the guerrillas," and continues walking up towards us.

His face was disfigured with rage, or was he going to cry? In one moment, as if catapulted by bitterness, he reached to his belt and drew his pistol. Days later we found out from the newspaper that his attempt at

97

freeing the hostages was a failure, that six of his men were wounded, that they were "waylaid" by a recently dynamited road, a trail planted with landmines. Does that justify what he did? His temperament was well-known, *Berrío the nutter*, his men called him behind his back. He aimed at the group and fired; someone fell beside us, but no-one wanted to know who it was, all of us hypnotized by the figure who still had us in his sights, now from a different angle, and was shooting, twice, three times. Two fell, three. The soldiers were surrounding Berrío now, in time, and he put his pistol in its holster and turned his back, jumping into the jeep and retreating from the plaza, further back into town, in the same direction the ambulance had gone. I thought Father Albornoz had been quite right to flee. There was no time to ask among ourselves, to corroborate that it was true and not one of so many ridiculous things that happened: in less than five minutes the ambulance erupted into the plaza and pulled up beside us.

They began to put the wounded inside, the last of whom was Mauricio Rey, I discovered, unable to believe it; he seemed drunker than ever.

"I'm not going to die," he said to me. "I'm not going to give them that pleasure."

We all ran now, in different directions, and some,

like me, left and came back to the same place, without a word, as if we didn't know each other. That was when I remembered Otilia and stood still. I looked around. A tremendous explosion was heard at the edge of the plaza, at the very heart of town: the greyish cloud of smoke faded and now I saw no-one; only a dog came out of the dust cloud, limping and howling. I looked for the men again: there was no-one. I was alone. Another explosion, a louder echo still swayed in the air, on the other side of the plaza, towards the school. So I headed for the school, sunk in the worst premonition, thinking that only there could I find Otilia, in the place most threatened by the combat, the school. If Otilia had thought to look for me at the presbytery, why would she not go to the school?

"Where are you going, *profesor*?" Señora Blanca shouted to me from the half-open door. I could only see a fraction of her white, shaken face. "Come and hide, but hurry."

I approached the presbytery, undecided. The shooting intensified, far and near. Now a group of soldiers ran past a few metres from me. One of the soldiers, who seemed to be running backwards, bumped into me, banging my shoulder; he made me stumble; I was about to hit the ground. This is how I arrived at the wide-eyed, white face.

"To look for Otilia," I said.

"She must be at home by now, waiting for you. Do not put yourself at risk, *profesor*. Come in right now, or I'll close the door. Listen to the shooting."

"What if Otilia is at the school?"

"Don't be stubborn."

Again I deplored my memory: I remembered that Rey told Otilia that I was at the Brazilian's house. So that's where I went, while I heard Señora Blanca's shouts, scolding me.

"You're going to get yourself killed," she yelled.

I saw when I arrived that the gate to Geraldina's house was closed, with a lock and chain, as was the door. The door to my house too: fastened with the latch, from the inside; I began hammering on the door, in vain, shouting to be let in. I was struck by the thought that if Otilia was inside she would already have opened the door, and I preferred not to think any further. It was possible that she simply did not hear me. Was Sultana's daughter still there, or had she gone?

I hear sobs, inside.

"It's me, open up, hurry."

No-one answers.

On the corner, not far from where I am − my forehead pressed against the door, hands raised, resting on the wood — another group of soldiers appears. They are not soldiers, I discover, tilting my head slightly. There are seven, or ten of them, in camouflage uniforms, but they're wearing jungle boots, they are guerrillas. They have seen me as well leaning against the door, and they know I am looking at them. They are coming towards me, I think, and then a shot from the opposite direction shakes them and captures their full attention: they run that way, crouched down, pointing their rifles, but the last of them stops for a second and during that second turns to look at me as if he wanted to say something or as if he recognized me and was about to ask if I were me, but he has not said a word, he does not speak, is he going to speak to me? I make out the sallow, young face, as if through fog, the eyes two black ignited coals; his hand goes to his belt and then he tosses, gently, in a curve, something that looks like a stone. A grenade, my God, I scream to myself, am I going to die? We both watch in suspense the trajectory of the grenade, which falls, bounces once and rolls like any other stone three or four metres from my house, without exploding, exactly in between Geraldina's door and mine, at the edge of the pavement.

The boy looks at it for a second, ecstatic, and speaks at last: I hear his voice filling the street like a celebration.

"Hey, it's your lucky day, Granddad, buy yourself a lottery ticket."

Naively I think that I should respond in some way, and I am about to say: "Yes, that was lucky, wasn't it?" but he has already gone.

Then my front door opens. Behind it is Sultana's daughter, crying.

"What about my mum?" she asks. "Should I go and look for my mum?"

"Not yet," I say.

I go in and close the door. I am still thinking about the grenade that did not explode. It is possible that it will explode now, that it will destroy the front of the house, or the whole house. I run inside, out into the garden. From there too you can hear gunfire, explosions. I walk back up the hallway, followed everywhere by the crying girl, and go into my room; I see myself leaning down to look under the bed, I go back out to the garden, look in the kitchen, in the room that used to belong to our daughter, I go into the bathroom.

"And Otilia?" I ask. "Has Otilia been here?"

No, she says, and repeats no, shaking her head, crying the whole time.

We have been going from one side of the house to the other, depending on the blasts, fleeing from wherever we hear them, engulfed in their frenzy; we end up behind the living room window, where we catch astonished, fitful glimpses of the fighting troops, without distinguishing which army they belong to, the faces as cruel as any; we are aware of them going past, ducked down, slowly or at full speed, shouting or dumb with desperation, and always the sound of boots, panting, curses. A louder bang shakes us, from inside the garden, the octagonal living-room clock – its face of painted glass, an Alka-Seltzer promotion that Otilia bought in Popayán – has split into a thousand lines, the hour stopped forever at five o'clock on the dot. I run down the hallway to the back door, not caring about the danger; what difference can it make when it seems the war is going on in my own house. I find the fountain – of polished sandstone – blown apart; on the ground shiny with water the orange fish still quiver; what to do? Pick them up? What will Otilia think – I wonder foolishly – when she finds this mess? I gather up the fish one at a time and throw them into the sky, far away, so Otilia will not see her fish dead.

At the back, the wall that separates my property from the Brazilian's smokes where it has been blasted in half: there is a breach the size of two men, there are pieces of the ladder scattered all over; flowers lie strewn about, their clay pots pulverized; half the trunk of one of the orange trees, split lengthwise, still trembles and vibrates like a harp, coming apart inch by inch; there are piles of smashed oranges, sprinkled like a strange multitude of yellow drops all over the garden. And that is when I discover, unable to believe my eyes now, the dark silhouettes of four or six soldiers who jog along balancing on the top of the wall. Soldiers? I ask myself. Yes, the same. They jump into my garden, pointing their rifles at me; I smell the sweat, their breath, one of them asks me where the door to the house is; I point out the route and run behind them down the hall. We hear Cristina's scream in the living room; she holds her hands over her face, thinks they are going to kill her.

One of the soldiers, the last one – the one closest

to us – seems to recognize her. I see that he looks at her with excessive attention.

"Hide under a table," he tells her, "get down on the floor," and carries on advancing behind the others.

I know I have to tell them something, warn them of something, ask them about something, but I do not remember anything. So we go to the door, which they open stealthily. They lean out, peer this way and that and burst onto the street.

"Close that door," they shout at me.

I close it, what was it I had to say to them? The grenade, I remember, but another tremendous blast – again from the direction of the garden   distracts me.

"Didn't you hear?" I say to Cristina. "Hide."

"Where?" she asks with a shriek.

"Wherever," I shout back. "Under the ground."

The smoke spreads from the garden, it is a long asphyxiating cloud that streams into the hallway. I return through its folds to the garden; I make out the edge of the wall, examine it: it is very possible that someone is following the soldiers, and in their place will find me; it does not matter, it is better to die at home than in the street. I remember Otilia and a sort of fear and rage inspire me to step right into the breach in the wall, as if that would protect me. The smoke is coming from another of the trees, burnt and split from the top; further down, on the very white pulp of the trunk stripped of its bark, I see a bloodstain, and, on top of the roots, pierced with splinters, the corpse of one of the cats. I clutch my head, everything spins around me, and in the middle of it all Geraldina's house shines in front of me, with no wall: this hole is a huge irony, through which I can take in Geraldina's garden in its entirety, the terrace, the round pool; and not just look, I could pass through to the other side; what am I thinking? Of Geraldina undressed, oh God. Is Otilia in there? I do not see anyone on the other side, I cannot distinguish anything. There are shots coming from the street, with increasing intervals between them. Far away, in a vortex of screams, the centre of which is the white point of the church, curls of smoke can be seen, on all sides. I enter my neighbour's garden, which has not suffered as much damage as mine – except for the absence of the macaws, their laughter, their strolls, although I soon find them, stiff, floating in the pool. I cross the terrace and proceed inside.

The glass door is wide open.

"Is there anyone here?" I ask. "Otilia, are you here?"

Something or someone moves behind me: I turn to look with my heart in my mouth. Our two hens are sheltering in the Brazilian's garden, as indifferent as they are extraordinary, luckier than the macaws; they peck patiently around the ground. They remind me of Maestro Claudino, of my promise.

I find Geraldina in the living room where I'd spoken to her not long before. She is still sitting in the same armchair, still dressed in black, still sunk in her sorrow, in a shadow of love made more all-encompassing, urgent and devastating than ever by sadness. Her hands in her lap, her eyes gone, a tall icon of suffering. Probably because it is dusk, and because it is war, the same deep darkness of this day surrounds everything more forcefully. I find other sitting spectres around Geraldina; women saying the rosary, their voices ask and answer in whispers. I interrupt the prayer. They ignore me. In vain I search for Otilia's face among them. I feel sorry for myself: if Otilia was praying with them she would already have come to meet me.

"And Otilia?" I ask in spite of everything.

They continue their muttered praying.

"She was here, sir," Geraldina's emotionless voice says to me. "She was here, and she left again."

I have returned to my house again, by the same route. I start to make coffee in the kitchen, and stay there, sitting, waiting for the water to boil in the pot. I listen to the water boiling, and remain still. The water evaporates completely, the pot burns; the thin strip of smoke rises up from the bottom of it and reminds me of the burnt tree, the dead body of the cat. Well, I was unable to make coffee; I turn off the stove, what time is it? How much time has passed? I do not hear any more shooting. How will time pass, my time, from now on? The din of the war disappears: now and then a distant lament, which seems almost not to belong to us, a call, a shouted name, any name, running footsteps, indistinct noises that fade and are replaced by absolute silence. Night is falling, shadows begin to hang everywhere, I can see nothing but myself. I try again to make coffee: I hold the small pot under the tap. All of a sudden there is no water, or electricity; you have wasted your chance to make coffee, Ismael, and who knows when the water and power will come back on? What would Otilia do in my position? She would fill the pot with water from the fountain, light the coal stove, she would ennoble the world, offering us coffee in the midst of catastrophe; I sit still, night arrives in full and I hear that someone is speaking out in the street, through a megaphone.

We are asked to bring any wounded out immediately, otherwise to remain inside our houses until the situation is stabilized, that is what the impersonal voice says through the megaphone:

"...until this situation is stabilized. We have succeeded in driving back the bandits."

I hear, as the only reply, a moan from inside the house. *Cristina*, I say to myself. Her name is the only thing that shakes me from this death-like paralysis into which I have sunk. I look in the kitchen drawers for a candle to light. I do not find one. I have to feel my way through my own house; I go to my room – the room Otilia and I share with that old wooden Saint Anthony, a sort of altar where the candles and matches are kept. The moan sounds again in the darkness; it has to be the girl, but she is not in the room. My hands tremble, light the candle with difficulty. With this flame I go through the house searching, calling Cristina.

I discover that she has gone into the room that used to be our daughter's, where I have not been for years – only Otilia goes in there, to pray for us.

"Here we will be closer to our daughter," she said.

"Cristina," I call out loudly "Are you injured?"

"No," she answers at last, coming out from under the bed.

With all that has happened and the unfortunate circumstances I deplore my own self, detesting myself for noticing, voluntarily or involuntarily, the bunched up dress, the pale bird-like thighs, the wild darkness between her legs, in the faint candlelight, her face wet with tears.

"What about my mum?" she asks again in terror.

She hugs an old teddy bear that used to belong to my daughter. She is a little girl: she could be my granddaughter.

"If you want, go out and look for her," I say. "And if you want to come back, come back, and if you don't want to, don't come back, but stop crying."

"How?" she managed to reply. "The tears just come out."

"This is no time to cry, Cristina. I'm not telling you to laugh, I'm just saying we have to gather our strength to find those we are looking for. If you cry, your tears weaken us."

I tell myself the same thing.

And I hear her leave the house, slam the door shut, run out into the night, the night that must stand just like the street: empty. I have stayed sitting on my daughter's bed, the candle in my hand, feeling the wax drip over my hands, the wick I extinguish with my fingers, smelling my own charred flesh, until dawn breaks. You have not returned, Otilia, not sooner and not later. I shall have to look for you again, but where, where did you go to look for me?

I hear birdsong – they sing in spite of everything. The garden appears to my eyes to be divided by gauzes of light, it is a haggard dawn, I hear the surviving cats meowing in the kitchen. I do what Otilia would do: I feed them bread and milk, and I eat the same thing, I am your other cat, I think, and in thinking it I remember the dead cat: I will have to bury that cat, so you shall never see your cat dead, Otilia. I go to the tree: the mangled cat is still there; I bury him under the same tree. Maestro Claudino's hut is the last place left, the last place you could have gone looking for me, Otilia, I told you myself I planned to take the Maestro a chicken; there you are, I shall find you there, and so there I go, repeating it to myself with all the force and stubbornness of a light in the middle of the fog that men call hope.

But first I go and look for and chase – in the Brazilian's garden – one of the hens, my hens, who have decided to keep on living in the neighbours' garden. I am aware of Geraldina's eyes watching me through the glass door, Geraldina dressed in mourning watches me in shock as I catch a hen at last and stuff it into a shoulder bag, laughing now: we shall have a chicken stew, Otilia, Maestro Claudino and I. Through the hole in the wall I return to my house, forgetting to wave to Geraldina, without saying goodbye. As I walk down the first empty streets I forget the war entirely: I feel only the warmth of the hen against my side, I believe only in the hen, its miracle, Maestro Claudino, Otilia, the dog, in the hut, all focused on the happy stew in the pot, far from the world and further still: on the blue invulnerable mountain in front of me, half hidden in the veils of fog.

The last house, on the paved street, just before the beginning of the highway, is Gloria Dorado's. Small, but big enough, clean, mango trees in the yard, it was a gift from Marcos Saldarriaga. I thought I saw Gloria for a second, standing at the open door, in white pyjamas, with a broom in her hand: she was going to say something to me, I thought, but she closed the door. She was going to say good morning and changed her mind and rightly so, I suppose, when she saw me laughing to myself, very discordant to the anguish with which she has lived since the disappearance of Saldarriaga. I have started off down the road when I hear her voice behind me, the voice of Gloria Dorado, the strange blue-eyed, brown-skinned woman Saldarriaga was devoted to.

"Be careful, *profesor*. We don't yet know whose hands the town is in."

"Whoever they belong to, they're the same hands," I say, and take my leave and carry on.

How good to get away from San José, full to the brim with solitude and fear, so sure am I of finding Otilia up on the mountain.

Far from town, near the bridle path, when night has still not quite separated from dawn, three shadows emerge from the bushes and jump out at me, surround me, too close, so close I cannot see their eyes. It is not possible to tell if they are soldiers – or whose, whether from here, or there, or from the other side, does it matter? Otilia is waiting. Something like the smell of blood paralyses me. I ask myself: have I even forgotten the war? What is wrong with me? Too late I regret not having listened to Gloria Dorado: *in whose hands are we*; I should have gone back home, and what about Otilia?

"Where do you think you're going, old man?"

They press against me, grip me, the point of a dagger at my stomach, the coldness of a gun at my neck.

"I'm going to get Otilia," I say. "She's just up here, on the mountain."

"Otilia," they repeat.

And then, one of the shadows: "Who is Otilia, a cow?"

I thought the other shadows were going to laugh at the question but the silence continues, oppressive, insistent. I believed it was a joke, and thought it best amid the laughter to make my escape with my hen. It was a serious question. They really wanted to know if I was talking about a cow.

"She is my wife. I am going to find her, up there, on the mountain."

"A stone's throw," says one of the shadows. He has put his face in my face, his cigarette breath covers me: "Haven't you heard? You can't just leave any time you want. Go back where you came from."

They are all still crushed together, pinning me.

"I did not hear," I tell them. "I am going to get my wife from Maestro Claudino's place."

"What maestro? What Claudino?"

Another shadow whispers in my ear, his bitter breath dampens the side of my head.

"Be thankful we're letting you go back where you came from. Stop fucking around and turn back, don't get on our nerves."

The other shadow comes closer and looks into the bag.

"What have you got there?" With a bandaged finger he half opens the shoulder bag. He looks me straight in the eye: "What is your business?" he asks, solemnly.

"I kill chickens," I reply. I still do not know why I answered that way, because of the stew?

The other two shadows look in.

"And nice fat ones," says one of them.

Nearby, so near, at the edge of the road, begins the bridle path that climbs the mountain. Otilia is waiting for me up there, I feel it. Or I want to feel it. Only now do I realize how exposed I am on this road, at daybreak, just us: *them and me*. I hear, I see a gust of wind that lifts small waves of dust among the stones; is it that I am going to die, at last? A desolate cold, that seems to have run straight down the bridle way and flowed out in front of us, guided by the wind, startles me, makes me think that no, Otilia is not up there, makes me think of Otilia for the first time without hope.

"Keep the hen," I say.

They snatch her out with one swipe.

"This guy's saved himself," shouts one of them, laughing.

"I'll wring its neck right now," says another. "I could scoff it whole."

They run to the other side of the road: they don't even look at me, and I head up the path. It starts to dawn on me that the hen is lost. At the first bend in the trail up the mountain I stop.

I shout at them, cupping my hands round my mouth, through the foliage: "I only kill chickens."

And I kept shouting this, repeating it – flanked by fury and fear, without the stew I had been dreaming of – "I only kill chickens."

The panic, the regret at having shouted drives me to run uphill, flee with all my strength, paying no mind to my pounding heart. I was asking them to kill me, but hunger must have been stronger than the desire to chase and kill me for shouting at them that I only kill chickens. It did not matter, in the end: I was only thinking of Otilia.

As soon as I arrived at the hut the fierce silence showed me what it had to show me. Otilia was not there. The body of Maestro Claudino was there, decapitated; at his side the dog's corpse, curled up in the blood. They had written on the walls with charcoal. *Collaborator.* Without trying, my gaze found the Maestro's head, in a corner. Like his face, his *tiple* guitar was also smashed against the wall: there was no need to take it down, I thought, absurdly, and the only thing I screamed at that moment was *Otilia*, her name. I walked around the cabin several times, calling her.

It was the only place I had left.

Finally I walked down to the road: the smell of the roasted chicken wafted on the air. Vomit rose to my teeth, and there, right by the side of the highway, in front of the smoke from the bonfire that encircled bushes across the road, I threw up what I had not eaten, my bile. Now they will kill me, I thought, as I walked quickly down the road, entirely out of breath, but I wanted to run because I still thought I would find Otilia in town, looking for me.

It seemed like any old Sunday in San José, well into the morning: *Everyone is going where they're coming*, I said to myself idiotically, because none of the faces I passed along the way was Otilia's.

Gloria Dorado again, at the edge of town, said wordlessly: "Have faith."

Not far from the road, fifty metres away, in the town's water tank, some soldiers were bathing; they were washing their clothes, joking with each other.

Near the plaza, men's voices come from the rectangular building that used to be the market, arguing, proposing, rejecting. Someone speaks through a megaphone. I go in but the quantity of bodies crowded into the corridor keeps me from getting very far. There I feel the midday heat for the first time. I listen to the discussion, I even distinguish, at the back of the room, in the centre of all the heads, the heads of Father Albornoz and the Mayor.

Professor Lesmes is speaking: he proposes vacating the municipality "so the military and the guerrillas find the scene of battle empty".

Voices reply in shouts, murmurs. Some think they should barricade the highway as a protest until the government moves the police out of San José.

"Yes," says Lesmes, "they should at least take their fortifications out of the urban centre to stop the assaults on the town."

They announce that the attack has left five soldiers, three policemen, ten insurgents, four civilians and one child dead, and at least fifty wounded. There is no consensus in the meeting, and what does it matter to me? I don't see Otilia either; I want to leave, but the compact group of recent arrivals behind me blocks me; in vain I try to make my way through; we are all sweating, we regard each other dumbfounded.

The Mayor dismisses the proposals; he will ask the national government to initiate a dialogue immediately with those who have taken up arms.

"We have to get to the roots of this problem," he says. "Yesterday it was in Apartadó, in Toribío, now in San José, and tomorrow in some other town."

"They want the town vacated," Father Albornoz

interrupts. "They have let me know."

"We cannot leave," several men reply heatedly. "People here have what little they have by the sweat of their brows and we are not going to throw it away."

"Evacuation is not the answer," the Mayor determines, and, nevertheless, it is not possible to ignore the deep alarm about another imminent assault on the town centre: who would have thought that it would happen to us as well, they say here, they say there, they repeat.

Years ago, before the attack on the church, displaced people from other towns used to pass through our town; we used to see them crossing the highway, interminable lines of men and children and women, silent crowds with neither bread nor destinations. Years ago, three thousand indigenous people stayed for a long while in San José, but eventually had to leave due to extreme food shortages in the improvised shelters.

Now it is our turn.

"My house has been turned upside down," someone shouts. "Who's going to pay for that?"

Disconsolate laughter is heard.

Father Albornoz begins a prayer.

"In the Lord's goodness," he says. "Our Father, who art in heaven . . ."

The laughter stops. I think of Otilia, my house, the dead cat, the fish, and, a moment later, while the prayer goes on, I manage at last to get out as if held up by all the bodies, which push me to the door; does nobody want to pray?

Outside we hear the cry of Hey, the empanada vendor: the echo bounces along the boiling street. Mechanically, I walk in the direction of the plaza. A group of men, several acquaintances among them, fall silent when I approach. They greet me anxiously. They are talking about Captain Berrío, temporarily relieved of his command while an investigation gets under way.

"They'll court martial him, and he'll end up a colonel in another town, as a reward for shooting civilians," predicts old Celmiro, older than me, and such a good friend that he avoids looking me in the eye.

Why are you frightened to see me, Celmiro? You feel sorry for me, for yourself, but in any case you decide to go home, surrounded by your children.

Voices warn me that landmines have been laid around the town: it will be impossible to leave town without the risk of being blown to bits, where were you, *professor*? All the outskirts of San Jose have been mined during the night, they've deactivated seventy or more devices, but how many remain? Damn, say the voices, there are tin cans, milk churns full of shrapnel and excrement, to infect the victims' blood, what bastards, what arseholes; the voices speak of Yina Quintero, a fifteen-year-old girl who stepped on a mine and lost her left ear and eye. Those who came into San José cannot now leave, they say, and nor do they want to go.

"I am going to the hospital," I tell them.

We hear a helicopter. We all look up, in suspense: now there are two helicopters, and we stand listening to them for a while, seeing them disappear in the direction of the garrison.

I walk away.

"*Profesor*," someone warns me, a voice I do not recognize: "They killed everyone in the hospital including the wounded. You keep looking for your wife: we know you're looking for her. She is not among the dead, which means she's still alive."

I have stopped, without turning my head.

"Missing," I say.

"Missing," the voice confirms.

"And Mauricio Rey?"

"Dead, like all the wounded. They even killed Dr Orduz, didn't you hear? This time he tried to hide in the refrigerator where they keep the medicine, and they found him: they riddled the fridge with bullets, with him inside.

I keep walking, not knowing where to.

"It was brutal, *profesor.*"

"You keep calm and wait," says another voice.

"They'll let you know."

"You need to keep calm."

I return again to my house, again I sit on the bed.

I hear the surviving cats meowing, circling around me.

Otilia is missing, I tell them.

The Survivors sink the abysses of their eyes into my eyes, as if they were suffering with me. How long has it been since I cried?

Three months after that last incursion into our town, three months exactly – because since then I count the days – the Brazilian's son arrived home, without anyone knowing who brought him, or how. He turned up at seven in the evening, alone, and gazed at his mother, motionless, speechless, standing like a statue in the doorway. She ran to embrace him, cried, he remained as if asleep with his eyes open, gone for good, and has not been anything but silent since then. Gaunt, skinnier than he had ever been, because he had never been thin and now he was skin and bones, he looked like a child pushed by force into old age: inscrutable and timid, he does nothing but sit, receive food, listen without listening, look without looking, every morning he wakes and every night he sleeps, he does not respond to any voice, not even his mother's, the anguished Geraldina in mourning. In his shirt pocket she found a note sent by his captors, where they specified which front they belonged to, with whom Geraldina had to deal and what price they were demanding for the Brazilian's life – Gracielita was not even mentioned.

Geraldina began to live as if petrified in fear: she was ordered not to give any details of the instructions to anyone, under threat of her husband's immediate execution. Overwhelmed, unable to decide to act, she could not help but confide her tragedy to Hortensia Galindo and me, who were with her when her son appeared, and who did not know how to help, what solution to propose, what to do, because the same thing was happening to all three of us, to me with the aggravating factor of receiving no news of Otilia – my Otilia without me, both of us without each other. Geraldina confined herself to waiting for the arrival of a brother, from Buga, who "will help her". Now all her preoccupation is focused entirely on her son so reserved he almost seems dead; in vain she attempts to wake him from the nightmare he is in: she hovers around him every minute of the day, hanging on his every gesture, and falls back desperately on a kind of game of deluded songs, in which she uselessly tries to convince herself that he participates, he, a child who seems mummified, stuck in an urn. She thought of taking him to Bogotá, to see some specialists, but the idea of distancing herself from the region where her husband was held prisoner put her off. The young doctor, who had been assigned to our town to fulfil her year of rural service, one of the few survivors of the attack on the hospital, has told her – in an attempt to calm her – that the delicate trance her son is in can only be remedied with time and tranquillity: and yes, the uncertainty that reigns in San José is perhaps similar to tranquility, but it is not the same; people go home early; the few businesses still here open for the morning and a couple of hours in the afternoon; then doors close and San José agonizes in the heat, it is a dead town, or almost, just like us, its last inhabitants. Only the dogs and the pigs sniff around the stones, the vultures flap their wings on the tree branches, the eternally indifferent birds seem to be the only ones not to notice this living death. Because once again we are newsworthy; the death toll goes up daily: after the attack, among the ruins of the school and the hospital, more corpses appeared: Fanny, the caretaker, with grenade shrapnel through her neck, and Sultana García, Cristina's mother, who was found riddled with bullets under a pile of bricks "with the broom still in her hands", people commented with bitterness. Realizing I was with them, hours before their deaths, leaves me suddenly stunned, whatever I do, alone or in company, dead to Otilia; the thought that she might show up the way they did makes me open my mouth like an idiot, open my arms as if waving away ghosts, open my eyes wider as if I myself were thinking right that very moment I am going mad at the edge of this cliff and feeling that a hand could push me at the most unexpected moment, at this very moment, now.

More landmines have exploded, or "were heard" – another thing people said – on the outskirts, fortunately without human victims, for now; only an anti-explosives dog (he was buried with military honours), a stray dog, two pigs, a mule, and an army truck, without casualties. It is extraordinary; we seem besieged by an army that is invisible and more efficient for it. No doctor has yet arrived to replace the deceased Gentil Orduz, nor has another lucid drunk resembling Mauricio Rey staggered through the streets. Lesmes and the Mayor travel to Bogotá, their requests for the front line to be pulled back from San José are not listened to. Otherwise, war and famine adapt themselves, more than willingly. The hundreds of hectares of coca planted around San José in the last few years, the "strategic location" of our town, as those in the know classify us in the newspapers, have made of this territory what the protagonists of the war also call "the corridor", dominion over which they fight for tooth and nail, and which causes the war to surface in everyone's very pores: this is what people talk about in the street, in furtive hours, and they talk in words and curses, laughter and laments, silence, invocations. I miss the conversation, and I am not going to deny it, of Dr Orduz and of Mauricio Rey, because Father Albornoz has also decided to die – in his way: leaving San José in the company of his sacristan, without saying goodbye – in his place came a priest more frightened than unfamiliar, recently ordained, Father Sanín, from Manizales.

Chepe was not spared either in the squall of death. They did not kill his pregnant wife, this is true, but they took her: she was in the hospital, for a routine check-up, when the attack started. They slipped Chepe a note under his door: *You, sir, have a debt to clear with us, and that's why we're taking your pregnant wife. We have Carmenza and need fifty million for her and another fifty for the baby on its way. Don't try to get round us again.* The news of this double kidnapping was soon in the newspaper, under the headline: *BABY ANGÉLICA KIDNAPPED BEFORE BIRTH.* Chepe himself, in an interview, candid in his pain, had revealed to the journalist the name they planned to give their daughter. The journalist, a young redhead covering the recent attack on San José, does not only publish her articles in the newspaper, but also conducts live interviews for a television news programme. Escorted by two officers, as well as her cameraman, she arrived in San José in one of those helicopters meant to evacuate seriously wounded soldiers – and dead ones – to their places of origin. She was granted this military dispensation because she is the niece of General Palacios. She has been strolling around for days under the sun, which at this time of year is intense, her ginger locks adorned with a white straw hat, her eyes hidden behind a pair of dark sunglasses. This morning I saw her pass by my door: she stopped for a moment, seemed doubtful; she looked at her cameraman as if questioning him; the young man looked impatient. The journalist was probably wondering whether I, an old man sitting alone by his house, was a good subject for a photograph. She decided I was not and carried on walking. I recognized her: I had seen her on the television at Chepe's. Being here, in this town, sunburnt, did not seem very agreeable to her. She continued her meandering through the blown-up streets, the wrecked houses. Slowly, her green T-shirt soaked in sweat – down the back, between her breasts – she seemed to be walking through hell, her mouth twisted in torment.

"Thank God we're leaving tomorrow, Jairito," I heard her say to her cameraman.

I had left my house, at dawn, to sit by the side of the door, as Otilia always did when she was waiting for me. I could still see the fog in the sunshine, persistent, this disaster that I do not know why those of us who remain seem determined to ignore. Thinking of Chepe and his pregnant wife, wondering how they managed to take her, how they transport people as fat as Saldarriaga, forcing them to walk up and down hills for kilometres, helps me to walk. I should go and keep Chepe company. Better to listen to someone than to sit here confirming Otilia's absence.

It is eight o'clock in the morning and I arrive at his shop. Some people are sitting beside him, at one of the tables in the aisle, in complete silence; they are drinking coffee. Others, here and there, are drinking beer, or smoking. There is no music. Chepe nods hello. I sit down with him, across from him, in an uncomfortable chair, which wobbles.

"So, that means they'll kill her," Chepe says to me. He stares at me for too long – is he drunk? – and shows me a note, which I do not take, but the contents of which I give him to understand I already know. "Where am I going to get that kind of money?" he asks me. "Damn it, *profesor*, where?"

What can I say? We remain silent. The girl who wore a daisy in her hair brings me a cup of coffee. She no longer has the daisy and her face is sombre. She resents, perhaps, my lingering look. She walks away unhappy. She does not hear us any more, like before, does not want to hear us. I find aguardiente bottles under the table.

"Where?" Chepe asks us all.

We do not know whether he has started to laugh or to cry, but his mouth slackens, his head trembles.

"Tell them just that, Chepe," they say to him.

"Negotiate with them, negotiate. That's what everyone does."

I see, behind Chepe, several neighbours' heads; some smile in silence, on the verge of a joke, because in spite of the bullets and splashes of blood there is always someone who laughs and makes the rest laugh, at the expense of death and the disappearances. This time there was just a touch of somewhat kind irony: Chepe's tears look like tears of laughter.

He recovers. It is as if he swallows his tears.

"And you, *profesor*? Any word about your wife?"

"Nothing."

"It won't be long, *profesor*, before they let you know," someone says. "They must be weighing up your treasures."

And someone else:

"*Profesor*, stop in at the post office. There were two letters for you."

"Really? So there's still post?"

"The world hasn't come to an end, *profesor*," says one of the ones who laugh.

"What do you know," I say. "Your world may not have ended, but mine has."

I finish my coffee, leave Chepe's shop, and head straight for the post office. Must be letters from my daughter, I think. When the church was blown up she wrote to us asking if we wanted to go and live with them, assuring us we would be welcomed by her husband, begging us to think of our grandchildren. Neither Otilia nor I had any hesitation: we were never leaving here.

Both letters are from my daughter. I do not read them in the post office, but return home, as if Otilia were waiting for me there, to read them. When I arrive I find several children crouched down in a circle, at the edge of the pavement. I ask them to let me past, but they stay where they are, their heads almost touching I lean over and see the children's hands, thin and tanned, stretched out towards the hand grenade. *The grenade*, I shout to myself. *It's still there*.

"Let me see," I say.

The oldest of the children makes up his mind, grabs the grenade and jumps back. The rest of the children jump back with him. I have frightened them. It is not possible, I think, putting my daughter's letters in my pocket. I'm going to blow up before reading your letters, María.

I reach out my hands, but the boy does not seem prepared to relinquish the grenade.

"It's not yours," he says.

The rest of them turn to look at me, waiting. They know very well that if they take off running I could never catch them.

"Nor yours," I say. "It's nobody's. Give it to me before it explodes, do you want to blow up like that dog they buried with honours?"

I plead inwardly that the boy had been among those who attended the funeral of the dog with military honours, on one side of the cemetery, when they played the cornets. And yes, he must know perfectly well what I am talking about because he immediately hands it over. That public burial was useful for something.

The other children take a few steps back, moving away from me but still surrounding me.

"Go on," I say to them. "Leave me alone with this."

They do not leave, they follow me – at a prudent distance, but following me – and where am I to go? I walk through the streets with a grenade in my hands, accompanied by children.

"Go away," I shout at them. "Don't follow me. This will blow us all up."

They carry on, unperturbed, and it even seems that more children come out of their houses, interrogate the first ones in whispers, and remain at my back, implacable. Where have so many children come from? Did they not leave?

At last I hear the terrified voice of a man.

"Throw that good and far away, *profesor*. What are you doing?"

Then the echo of another voice, a woman, shooing the children away.

"Go home," she yells.

The children do not obey. Silent, impassive, they are surely waiting to see an old man blow up in front of them, never supposing that they too would be blown up. The doors of more houses open, the woman's voice is now screeching.

I head straight for the cliff. I cross the street in front of Mauricio Rey's house, almost running. I stop at the edge of the cliff. Now the children come too close, one of them, the smallest one, naked from the waist down, is even holding on to my sleeve.

"Get away from here," I say.

Sweat forces me to close my eyes. I am sure that when I raise my arm and throw the grenade, just from the force I shall need to use to throw it, it will blow up in my hand and I will burst apart, surrounded by children, accompanied by a bunch of children; God knows, sooner or later someone in town will laugh about this: *When*

Professor Pasos blew up he took with him a good number of children,
I say to myself, noticing the hard surface of the grenade
in my hand, an animal with jaws of fire that will dissolve
me in a breath; if I were alone, at least, this would be
painless, I would no longer have to wait for you; Otilia,
did I not tell you that I would be the first to go?

The children remain behind me, I make one last and
vain attempt to get rid of them, I endeavour to scare
them with gestures, and, instead, they crowd closer
round me, voices of men and women call them from
afar. I raise my hand and throw the animal over the
cliff, we hear the bang, we are dazzled by the little
flashes leaping up from below, the colourful lights
that thunderously climb the branches of the trees, to
the sky. I turn to the children: their faces are happy,
absorbed – as if they were watching fireworks.

I return home, past the flushed faces of women; they
have only just heard and have come for their children;
some hug them, others scold them, spank them as if it
were their fault, I think, hearing that the men are questioning me, for now it is men and women who follow me.

"Where was that grenade, *profesor*?"

"On my street," and inside, I am riddled with a
shame I cannot yet admit: I forgot about that grenade
for months: the grass must have grown up around it,

136

covering it — I think, to justify myself — disguising it as a grey flower, burying it.

Men and women come home with me, and come in, as if into their own homes. What are we celebrating? Who have we defeated? It is better this way, it has been ages since anyone came into this house as if for an impromptu party; what if Otilia suddenly appeared from the kitchen? They congratulate me, someone chants my name, more people find out, in a minute; I only want to sit down and read my daughter's letters, but on my own. Impossible. Now Chepe arrives with those who were drinking at his café. One of them hands me a shot of aguardiente, which I drink down in one. People applaud. I notice my hand shaking: was I afraid? Of course I was afraid, I have wet myself, I discover, but not from fear, I repeat, it is old age, just old age — and I go into my room to change my clothes. There no shame invades me, it is not my fault that I have lost my memory, no old man is at fault for that, I tell myself. I have put on a fresh pair of trousers and stay like that, sitting on the bed, the letters in my hand. I recognize my daughter's handwriting again, but I want to read them alone, I shall have to see these friends out.

"What's the matter, *profesor?*" they call from the other side of the door. "Come out and see us," and they laugh and applaud when I come out. "*Profesor*, don't you have any music?"

The same children who found the grenade walk around the garden, probably looking for more grenades to prolong the party, admiring the tree split down the middle, the carbonized orange tree, the rubble of the fish pond, the withered flowers among the remains – Otilia will be sad when she comes back, because I forgot to water her flowers.

Several of the neighbourhood women take over the kitchen, they light the coal stove and make coffee for everyone.

"What do you live on, *profesor*? God will have to take pity on you, Otilia will be back, have faith, we pray for her every day."

The two Survivors, filled with fear, watch the crowd from the wall. Through the breach appears the black figure of Geraldina, accompanied by her dumbstruck son. Some of the ladies tell her about the grenade. Again I am offered a shot, which I drink again, in one gulp.

The truth is – I tell Chepe in secret, as if shouting – I would have liked to blow myself up, but alone.

"I know what you mean, *profesor*, I know what you mean," he tells me, with reddened eyes.

From the group of women Ana Cuenco and Rosita

Viterbo come forward and take me aside.

"*Profesor*, why don't you come home with us, with our families?" they ask me.

I tell them I do not understand.

"We beg you, *profesor*, we've got it all arranged, we're going today. In Bogotá you can wait for Otilia, from there things will seem clearer. Or go to your daughter's house, but go as soon as you can, leave this town."

"I am not leaving," I tell them. "It hadn't occurred to me."

After beating around the bush a little they say they want to buy, to take with them as a souvenir, our old wooden Saint Anthony.

"He is miraculous, and, in any case, we will take better care of him for Otilia than you can."

"Miraculous?" I say. "Well, he forgot to bring any miracles here," and I tell them they can have the wooden saint. "You can take it whenever you want."

They do not need to be told twice, they know their way. With extreme care, it seems to me, they disappear with the small statue of Saint Anthony, cradled in their arms like a baby, just when I start to have doubts and wonder whether Otilia would agree with my decision to give it to them, but I do not manage to call them: at that moment people make way for someone and pull back from me, as if pointing me out.

It is the young journalist, the cameraman, two officers.

"Allow me to congratulate you," she says, and holds out a soft hand, too soft, with which she gently pulls me to her. And she has given me a kiss on the cheek without letting go of my hand: it is the same smile she uses to begin her broadcasts.

The cameraman sets up his camera, leans for a moment over the instrument, presses one of the buttons.

"Just a couple of questions, *profesor*," she goes on saying.

She smells of soap, as if she had just bathed; why should the smell of soap on a woman unsettle me at this time? She is beautiful, her hair red and damp, the white hat in her hand, but she does not seem real, beside me. She and her cameraman strike me as otherworldly; what world do they come from? They smile with rare indifference; is it the dark sunglasses? They want to be quick, you can tell from the way they move, she says something else to me, which I do not hear, I do not want to listen, I make an effort to understand her, she is simply carrying out her work, she could be my own daughter working, but she could not be my daughter, I do not want to speak nor can I: I take a step back, with a finger I point to my mouth, once, twice, three times, indicating that I am mute.

She half opens her mouth, and looks at me in

disbelief, as if she is going to laugh. No. Something like indignation inspires her.

"What a rude man," she says.

"Today the teacher has decided to be mute," someone yells.

An explosion of laughter follows.

I go to my room, close the door, and there I stay, standing with my forehead resting against the wood, hearing the people gradually leave. The nearby mewing of the Survivors encourages me to come out. There is nobody in the house, but they have left the door open. What time is it? Unbelievable: it is nightfall. Not even hunger tells me the time any more. I have to remind myself to eat. I must have forgotten, surely, because there is no power. I go to the front door, out by the pavement, and sink into Otilia's chair, to wait for her, while I read María's letters in the last light of dusk. In both letters she tells us the same thing: to come and live with her, in Popayán, that her husband thinks so too, that he demands it. She asks that you write to her, Otilia, wonders why you have not written. Now I shall have to write for you. And what shall I tell her? I shall tell her that Otilia is unwell, that she cannot write and sends her greetings; it will be bad news – but with a scrap of hope, a thousand times better than telling her the worst is true, that her mother is missing. We still do not want to leave, I shall tell her; what should we leave for, at this stage? Those would be your own words, Otilia: but thank you for the offer and may God bless you, we will keep your support in mind, but will have to think about it: we need time to leave this house, time to leave what we have to leave, time to pack up what we need to take, time to say goodbye forever, time for time. If we have spent our whole lives here, why not a few weeks more? We are still hoping that the situation here will change, and if it does not change then we shall see, or we shall go or we shall die, as God wills, let God's will be done, whatever pleases God, whatever he feels like.

"*Profesor*, don't sleep in your chair."

A neighbour who I know that I know but do not recognize wakes me up now. He is carrying an oil lamp with the flame low: the yellowish beam illuminates us, in gusts, thick with mosquitoes.

"They're going to eat you alive," he says.

"What time is it?"

"It's late," he says tortuously, "late for this town; who knows whether it is for the rest of the world."

"It is," I say.

He does not take the hint. He hangs the lantern on the door handle and crouches down, leaning against the wall, removes his hat, using it as a fan, and reveals his shaved, sweaty head, scar across his forehead, tiny ears, blisters on the back of his neck. I must know who he is, but I do not remember, is it possible? I distinguish, in the half-light, that he has a lazy eye.

"Let's go in," I say. "We'll make some coffee in the kitchen."

I do not know why I say it, when in reality I want to go to bed and sleep, at last, in spite of the world – free of worry about disappearances, let them not bother me, I want to sleep unconscious – why do I say it when, furthermore, this man, whoever he might be in my memory, causes me an inescapable annoyance and unease; is it the way he smells of petrol, his tone of voice, that twisted way of expressing things?

Once inside the kitchen, when he sees me light a candle, he puts out his lamp, "to economize", he says, although we both know that candles are also scarce in this town. He kneels on the floor and starts playing with the Survivors. It is strange: the Survivors never let anyone except Otilia touch them, and now they are meowing, they coil happily around the man's arms and legs. He is barefoot, his feet dirty with dust and cracked mud: if I did not doubt my own eyes, floating in the shadows, I would say dirty with blood.

"You are the first person ever to invite me in for coffee in this town," he says, and, afterwards, sitting where Otilia sat, "in years."

While we wait for the coals to come back to life in the stove, for the water to boil, I feed the Survivors –

rice soaked in rice soup.

"*Profesor*, do you cook?"

"Yes. Enough."

"Enough?"

"Enough not to starve to death."

"But your wife used to cook and you only ate, right?"

That is how it was, I think. I turn to look at the stranger: unrecognizable; why do I lose my memory when I need it most? We drink in silence, sitting around the stove. I am grateful for the tiredness I feel. Tonight I shall be able to sleep, I hope not to dream, simply not to dream; if I had slept outside, in the chair, my back would hurt the next day; I shall sleep in bed and convince myself for a few hours that I am sleeping with you, Otilia: what hope.

However, the familiar stranger does not take his leave.

He is still there, even though we both emptied our cups in three gulps, even though there is no more coffee in the pot, in spite of this, in spite of everything – I get impatient. I have been friendly to him, after all he kept me from sleeping the whole night in the chair: Otilia would not have liked me to wake up outside in the street with the whole town looking at me.

"Well," I say, "I am going to have to say goodnight. I want to sleep, I hope once and for all."

"Is it true, *profesor*?" he asks, not giving a fig for my words. "Is it true that Mauricio Rey pretended to be drunk so they wouldn't kill him?"

"Who says that?" I answer, without managing to avoid the sort of rage I haven't been able to defeat since they took Otilia. "Mauricio really did drink. I don't think his bottles were full of water."

"No, of course, surely not."

"They smelled of pure alcohol."

We are silent again; why does he ask me that? Since when did they not kill drunks around here? They are the first ones they do kill, and it must be easy, for they are defenceless: the sober are the majority, Mauricio Rey used to say. The candle goes out and I am not going to replace it. We are almost in the dark. I hear him sigh as he lights his lamp and stands up. By the yellow, earthy light, which makes the kitchen a sort of shadow of flames, I see the Survivors have left, Otilia is not in the kitchen either, Otilia is nowhere.

Only when the stranger has left do I remember: it is Hey, the empanada vendor; what is he doing here? I should have told him, in spite of everything, to stay in my house, because at this hour, in such darkness, even with his lantern in his hand, he could easily be confused with someone who has to be killed. Why did I say he was annoying? An unfortunate fellow, what fault is it of his if he rubs everyone up the wrong way? I light a candle and go out of the door, in the hope of finding him – seeing him in the distance, calling him. The light of his lantern has disappeared.

I hear some moaning in the night, a little girl sobbing? Then silence, and then another cry, longer, almost a howl, very close to my house, by Geraldina's gate, which sways and creaks. I go over there, protecting the candle flame with my hand: I need not have bothered, there is not the slightest breeze, and the heat seems worse outside. The candle melts quickly

It is a girl, I discover, standing, leaning back against the railings, and, in front of her, rubbing her, a shadow that could be a soldier.

"What are you doing here, old man? What are you looking at?" says the soldier with a sigh, playing down the assault, and, since I stay where I am, still surprised at having found something so different from what I was imagining – I was thinking of groans of utmost agony – the light from the candle flares up, extending over us, and they stop, with the gesture of a single body blinded. In the light I make out the face of Cristina, Sultana's daughter, observing me with a frightened smile over the soldier's shoulder.

"What are you looking at?" the lad repeats as a threat. "Get lost."

"Let him watch," Cristina says all of a sudden, revealing much more of her sweaty face, studying me. "He likes to watch."

I notice from her voice that she is drunk, or drugged.

"Cristina," I say, "you're welcome to stay here whenever you want. There is a bed."

"Yeah, I'll be there in a minute," she says. "Right away, but with company."

She and the soldier burst out laughing, and I back away, staggering. I leave them, harassed by the gentle mocking that falls off, behind me, in the dark night. Thus I have returned to my house, to my bed – defeated by Cristina's harsh voice, by her words.

By candlelight I look at my shoes, take off my shoes, look at my feet: my toenails curl like hooks, my fingernails, too, look like they belong to birds of prey; it is the war, I tell myself, something of it is bound to stick, no, it is not the war, it is simply that I have not cut my nails since Otilia has not been here; she used to cut mine and I hers, so we would not have to bend over, remember: so we would not increase our aches, and I have not shaved either, or cut this hair that in spite of my age insists on not disappearing, one morning I noticed, one morning I looked in the mirror unintentionally and did not recognize myself:

Geraldina was right to look at me with apprehension the last time, deploring me, just like the rest of the people, men and women who for the last two months stop their conversations when I approach, look at me as if I have gone mad; what would you say, Otilia? How would you look at me? Thinking of you only hurts, sad to admit, and especially lying on my back in bed, without the living proximity of your body, your breathing, the imaginary words you spoke in your sleep. That is why I force myself to think of other things, when I try to sleep, Otilia, although sooner or later I talk to you and tell you things; only this way I begin to sleep, Otilia, after going through a stretch of my life without you, and manage to sleep deeply, but without resting.

I dream of the dead: Mauricio Rey, Dr Orduz; the conversation with Hey probably made me remember them as I fell asleep, and speaking out loud without noticing, as if you were listening to me, "What do you think of this life?" I tell an invisible Otilia. "Mauricio Rey and the doctor dead, and Marcos Saldarriaga probably still alive."

"Let those alive go on living," Otilia would say, I am sure, "and allow those who die to die. You keep out of it."

I can almost hear her voice.

On several occasions Marcos Saldarriaga referred to Dr Orduz as a guerrilla collaborator: perhaps that is why the paramilitaries wanted to capture him, to call him to account, or avail themselves of his services: his patients used to joke that Orduz knew how to use his scalpel like the best murderer. In any case the damage was done and threats against the doctor, whether direct or veiled, became constant, encumbering his life. People said, absurdly, that he lent out the hospital's cadavers for the purposes of transporting cocaine inside them, that he was a key figure in the contraband of weapons to the guerrillas, that the ambulances were at his personal disposal, and he filled them up with cartridges and rifles. Orduz defended himself with his imperturbable smile; he attended General Palacios, was a friend to soldiers and officers, no matter their rank;

no-one complained of his efficiency as a doctor. And, nevertheless, the damage was done, because no matter what the truth was, he would die in the fire of war.

A similar damage was done to Mauricio Rey, also thanks to Marcos Saldarriaga. They had been political enemies for many years, ever since Adelaida López, Rey's first wife, ran for Mayor. She was an enterprising woman and clear as day, as her slogans ran, and yes, as an exception to the rule, the slogans were true: clear as day, enterprising: perhaps for that very reason she was murdered with bullets and garrotte: four men, all carrying guns, one of them with a garrotte in his hands, knocked at Mauricio Rey's door: they asked his wife to come outside. They both refused. Night was beginning, and so was one of the most painful crimes in the memory of this municipality – as the newspapers pointed out – the men grew tired of waiting, they entered the house and took Adelaida out by force, along with Mauricio. The one with the garrotte began to punch the woman in the face while Mauricio was held face down with a gun to his head. Their only child, a thirteen-year-old girl, ran out after her parents. They shot the mother and daughter. The girl died instantly, while Mauricio picked his wife up in his arms and carried her to the hospital where she died minutes later, after the futile attempts of Orduz – who tried until the last moment to save her. Absurdly, since then, the friendship between the doctor and Mauricio has been irreparable, and all because Mauricio, in his bitter bouts of drunkenness, felt no compunction at lashing out and blaming the doctor, in an unjust but desperate way, calling him inept.

One of the murderers, arrested a few weeks later, admitted being a member of the regional Self-Defence Forces. He said that his bosses met on three occasions to plan the crime, because Rey's wife was making headway in her electoral campaign, and because she had publicly refused to have any rapprochement with the para-military organizations of the region: the plan involved one former congressman, two former mayors and a police captain. Although the murderer never mentioned Marcos' name, it was always thought that Marcos had something to do with the incident. That was why Rey never recovered from the crimes committed against his family and devoted himself to drinking non-stop, and at any moment of drunkenness he would remember that Marcos had defamed his wife on more than one occasion, and that he was guilty. Years later he married again, and even that did not save him from the memory; he could never understand why they did not kill him the day they killed his wife and daughter, although he realized that sooner or later they would try to get rid of him. Many people ridiculed him behind his back, saying that he pretended to be lost in drink to gain sympathy.

All these facts made Marcos Saldarriaga the invulnerable man of San José, because he seemed to have an understanding with the guerrillas, the paramilitaries, the army and the drug traffickers. That explained the origin of his money, which must have had multiple sources: he contributed large sums to Father Albornoz's humanitarian activities, he gave thousands to the Mayor, for charitable works – which according to Gloria Dorado the Mayor returned in kind – thousands to General Palacios, for his animal-protection programme, supplied uniforms and provisions for the soldiers of the garrison, organized colossal parties for them and started buying land from the peasant farmers, outrageously, by fair means or foul: he set the price, and any landowner who did not accept disappeared, until it was his turn to disappear, into who knows whose hands, those of which forces (the deceased Maestro Claudino, who was taken with him, never checked, never knew who they were, nor did he ask), the fact is that Saldarriaga disappeared leaving behind him a trail of hatred, for no-one, in the end, held him in any esteem – apart from his lover and his wife, possibly – not even his escorts and foremen, who instead of Saldarriaga called him Saldiarrhoea, which did not prevent, for four years, the whole town of San José showing up at Hortensia Galindo's house every 9 March, to regret his disappearance, to feast and to dance.

In my dream I seemed to be entering a house with no roof, where the doctor and Mauricio, on the patio, sitting across from each other, were talking; the wind in torrents blew down from above, like rivers, and prevented me from hearing what they were saying, and, nevertheless, I knew that it was something that concerned me alone, that at any moment my fate was to be decided, that in reality the two of them had me confused with someone else, with whom?

All of a sudden I understood: they both were convinced that I was Marcos Saldarriaga, and that was it: in a full-length mirror that suddenly sprang up beside me like a living being looking at me I saw myself with the face and body of Marcos Saldarriaga, the vast and detestable body.

"Who changed my body?" I said to them.

"Don't come near us, Marcos," they shouted, their voices almost physical, slapping against the wind.

"You're confusing me with Marcos," I told them, but they ordered me not to come near, they rejected me.

Other men came in, lots of them, strangers, armed shadows: they were coming for me, to eliminate me, and I could not hope for help from Rey, nor from the doctor, I *sensed* that to them I was the informer, the one who had marked them.

"I am not Marcos," I yelled, and the dead men – because in my dream as well the two of them were dead – insisted on confusing me with Marcos, or was I really Marcos Saldarriaga and waiting to be executed, without hope? It was my last doubt, the intolerable doubt of dreams, while Mauricio's voice and the doctor's voice rose, blaming me, and I still had not yet escaped their voices when Geraldina's voice came to liberate me.

"*Profesor*, wake up. You're shouting."

Dawn was breaking.

"*Profesor*, do not suffer so."

So this was true: there, before me, in the doorway, inside my garden, inside my house, inside my room, dressed in black, although at last with a sky-blue scarf on her head, Geraldina survived, and at her side her son, asleep on his feet.

"*Profesor*, I thought you were not at home. I was calling you from the garden, forgive me for bothering you."

"It was a nightmare."

"I realized, I heard you. You said you were not Marcos Saldarriaga."

"And I am not, am I?"

She looked at me, alarmed.

I got out from under the sheets; I had fallen asleep fully clothed. Sitting on the edge of the bed, I remembered that I was an old man when I bent over to look for my shoes: my clumsiness and a sudden sharp jab in the back paralysed me; she passed me my shoes, in the nick of time, because I could have fallen. I remained with my shoes in my hand; now would I not be able to put them on? Of course I would: Geraldina, Geraldina in my bedroom, waking me up, her apparition.

"You sleep under blankets" – she was astonished – "and so many. Don't you burn up with this heat?"

"Old age chills a person," I told her.

I imagined her sleeping, in spite of myself: naked, with no covers.

"Come and have breakfast with us, *profesor*, why do you never want to come and visit us any more?"

Why do I not want to? I do not know the answer, because I do not manage, or do not want, to confront it. I proceed behind Geraldina, trying in vain not to recognize her besieging scent, my eyes involuntarily exploring her black-clad back, and catching a glimpse, beneath the mourning, of her legs, her sandals, the radiant movement of her body, her whole life diffusing and proclaiming, beneath the veils of fatality she is suffering in this world, the perhaps inclement desire to be

156

possessed as soon as possible, albeit by death (by me?),
to forget the world for one moment, albeit for death.

For me.

Thus we proceed in silence, skirting the empty pool,
dirty with orange peel and pips, bird shit. I close my
eyes for a second, because I do not want to remember
Geraldina naked, because this must be why, more than
anything, I do not want to see her; it pains me, exhausts
me, hopeless in the midst of Otilia's disappearance, to
witness that my mind and my body are moved and
suffer for the mere presence of this woman alone in
the world, Geraldina, her voice or her silence, although
dressed in mourning, saddened, darkened – when it is
supposed that her husband has not died.

We sit at the table, before a dazzling china dinner
service; sunlight fills the kitchen. I suddenly discover
Hortensia, Marcos Saldarriaga's wife, there waiting for
us, like the continuation of the nightmare: she sits at
the head of the table, and, from the outset, speaks to
me in such pitiful tones, and sighs so much that now,
too late, I regret having accepted the invitation to
breakfast.

"Take care, *profesor*," she says, "not to be as untidy as
this when Otilia comes back." She stares at me for a
moment: "Because God will help her to come back. If

Otilia had died, they would have found her by now. That means she's still alive, *profesor*, everyone knows that." She reaches out and rests her small, fat, very pale hand on mine for an instant. "Look, I'll be frank with you: if they took my husband, who could not even walk he was so fat, twice as fat as I am" – here she smiles, upset – "then why couldn't they take Otilia, who wasn't, or isn't, pardon me, so old or so fat? Wait for news, it will come, sooner or later. They'll tell you how much they want. But while you wait, pay some attention to yourself, *profesor*. Why don't you cut your hair? Don't lose faith, don't forget to eat and to sleep, I know what I'm talking about."

The meal is served; it does not seem to be a normal breakfast, but rather lunch and dinner. The boy sits beside me, a faraway look in his eyes, gestures of the living dead: this is more terrible to see in him because he is a child.

Geraldina shows me the table.

"Look, *profesor*. Hortensia brought us these lobsters."

"Lobsters that were given to me," says Hortensia, as if excusing herself, and I see her mouth is watering. "They're a memento of a lunch with General Palacios. He was sent one hundred and twenty live lobsters for his birthday. Shipped from Canada, alive. I expect they travelled first class."

"And there's *plátano aborrajado, profesor,*" Geraldina interrupts. "I made this dish. You know, *profesor*, it's made with very ripe plantain, so black they ooze syrup; you fry them after filling them with cheese and dipping them in a batter of egg, milk and flour . . ."

"Just a black coffee," I say to Geraldina, "please."

I do not know what these women are talking about. I have not the slightest appetite. The only excuse I can find to hide my weariness of everything and everyone is to direct my attention to the boy, pretend to be concerned about him. After all, has my life not been spent surrounded by children, doing battle with them, sharing their sadness and their joy? Now I find myself with him. I remember him rolling around in his garden: he must have some memory of games, of happiness, why does he not speak? Enough time has passed. Is he not being spoilt, now? Would a reprimand not do him more good, a shout at least to wake him from his fantasy? He holds a piece of pineapple nougat, which he is about to eat. He has filled out again, he is as fat as he used to be, or maybe fatter.

I take the nougat out of his hand, to his great surprise, to his mother's surprise, and say to him: "What about Gracielita, where is she?"

He looks at me in shock, at last he looks at someone, I think.

" "Now then," I say, putting my face almost on top of his. "It's your turn to talk. What has become of Gracielita, what happened?"

The mere mention of Gracielita's name shakes him. He looks me in the eye, he understands me. Geraldina stifles a cry with her hand. But the boy still does not say a word, though he does not stop looking at me.

"And your father?" I ask him. "What happened to your father; how was he?"

The boy's eyes fill with tears: now all we need is for him to cry, and yes, it would be best, the lamentable excuse to get away from this ludicrous table. Then the child looks at the very fat Hortensia Galindo, who has paused, her hand on one of the lobsters. Then he looks for his mother, and finally seems to recognize her.

Then he says, as if he had learned it by heart:

"My daddy told me to tell you that we should both leave here that you should gather everything up and not wait one day that's what my daddy told me to tell you."

The two women gasp.

"Leave?" Geraldina is shocked. She has circled the table to come and hug her son. "Leave?" she repeats, and buries her face, her sobs, in her son's chest. But then she appears to think it over, while she looks at Hortensia and at me. She finds, surely (I see it in her hopeful eyes), reasons, and permission, to leave. "Thank you,

160

profesor, for getting him to speak," she stammers, and weeps without untangling herself from her son, which does not keep Hortensia from starting to eat.

I find the coffee pot. I pour myself a cup. I have waited a long time for this moment.

"Do you remember me?"

The boy nods. This time it is I who has a sinking feeling inside.

"Do you remember Otilia?"

He looks at me again as if he did not understand. I am not going to give up.

"You remember her, she gave you a coconut biscuit one morning. Later you came back and asked for another and she gave you four more, for your father, your mother, Gracielita, and the last one for you. You remember, don't you?"

"Yes."

"So you remember Otilia, then?"

"Yes."

"Was Otilia there where they took your father? Was Otilia with Gracielita, with you, with the hostages?"

"No," he says. "Not her."

The silence around us is absolute. My eyes stray unbidden to a lobster, encircled by rice, slices of plantain. I apologize to the women. I feel the same nausea as when I came down from Maestro Claudino's cabin.

161

I go back through the garden to my house, to the bed they had got me out of, and I stretch out on my back, as if I were ready to die, now, and alone, fulfilled, although the Survivors meow beside me, curled up on top of the pillow.

"What day is it?" I ask them. "I've lost track of the days. How many things have happened without our noticing?"

The Survivors leave the room and I am left more alone than ever, now definitively alone, it's true, Otilia, I have lost count of the days without you.

Monday? Another letter from my daughter. Geraldina brings it to me, accompanied by Eusebito. I do not open it. What for?

"I already know what she says," I explain to Geraldina, and shrug my shoulders, smiling to myself.

Yes. Smiling and shrugging my shoulders; why do I not read my daughter's ninth letter, even if just out of affection, although I know in advance what she says? She is asking about Otilia, and one day I shall have to answer her. Not today. Tomorrow? And what shall I tell her? That I do not know, I do not know. The letter slips from my hands, a dead thing, lands at my feet. We are in my garden, sitting in the middle of the rubble; Geraldina picks up the letter and hands it to me, I put it in my pocket, folding it.

Then the boy's face appears before me, he plants

himself in front of my eyes, like I did to him, at the table.

"You asked me about her," he says.

"Yes," I say. But who is she? And I find, very far away in my memory: *Gracielita*: the two children were prisoners.

The boy's face is stunned; it is a rapid memory, that terrifies Geraldina and me, without knowing exactly why.

"We were looking at a butterfly," he tells us. "The butterfly flew, behind, or around, we couldn't see it, it was gone.

"'I've just swallowed the butterfly,' she told me. 'I think I've swallowed it, get it out,' she said."

She opened her mouth all the way; she was someone else, disfigured by fear, her hands at her temples, her eyes popping in disgust, her mouth open wider and wider, an immense round darkness where he thought he could see the iridescent butterfly flapping its wings against a black sky, going further and further in. He put two fingers on her tongue, and pushed. Nothing else occurred to him.

"'There's nothing,'" I told her.

"'I've swallowed it then,' she screamed. She was going to cry."

He saw on her lips a film of the fine powder that detaches from butterflies' wings. Then he saw the butterfly crawl out of her hair, flutter a little and soar up to the other side of the trees, into the clear sky.

"'There's the butterfly,' I shouted. 'It only brushed you with its wings.'"

She caught sight of the butterfly as it disappeared. She held back her tears. With a sigh of relief she saw again that the butterfly was flying far away. It flew in front of the sun, far from here. Only then did they look at each other for the first time, and it really was as if they had just met — in captivity. A shared joke made them laugh: were they playing and tumbling in the garden, their faces together, not letting go of each other, as if they never wanted to be separated again, while the men were coming to take them? But he looked at his fingers, still wet from Gracielita's tongue.

"And Gracielita?" Geraldina asks her son, as if she had just realized, or understood at the last moment that all this time she had thought only of her son. "Why didn't they bring her?"

"She was going to come, they had put us both up on the same horse."

The boy's voice trembles, broken by fear, by bitterness.

"One of those men came and said he was Gracielita's uncle, and he took her. He made her get down off the horse, and took her."

"That's all we needed," I say to myself out loud, "Gracielita turning up here in a uniform, dealing out shots left and right, filling the town she was born in full of lead."

I burst out laughing, unable to hold back my laughter.

Geraldina looks at me in surprise, disapproving; she moves away, taking her son by the hand. They cross through the breach in the wall and disappear.

I keep laughing, sitting there, my face in my hands, uncontrollable. The laughter hurts my gut, my heart.

Thursday? Mayor Fermín Peralta cannot return to San José.

"I am under threat," he reveals, and no-one says specifically by whom.

Enough to know he is *still under threat*, what more? Not long ago his family left town, to be reunited with him. Now he deals with things from Teruel, a relatively safe town – compared to ours, with its landmines, and the reminder of war every now and then.

Professor Lesmes returned only to collect his things and say goodbye. We were with him, six or seven regulars, at Chepe's, sitting at the tables outside. Among us was Hey, distant but alert, a beer in his hand. Apparently, Lesmes had forgotten that Chepe's wife, and my own wife, had been kidnapped.

"Did you hear?" he asked us, almost happily. "They kidnapped a dog in Bogotá."

One or two smiled, amazed: was it a joke?

"I saw it on the news. Didn't you see it?" he asked us, not remembering that we, without electricity, no longer had access to television, and perhaps for that reason we chatted more, or sat in communal silences, for whole afternoons, at Chepe's.

By that point nobody was smiling.

"And what was this dog called?" asked Hey, strangely interested.

"Dundí," Lesmes told him.

"And?" Hey urged him on.

"A pure-bred cocker spaniel; what more do you want to know, the colour? The smell? It was pink, with black spots."

"And?" Hey continued, actually interested.

Lesmes looked resigned.

"He showed up dead," he said at last.

Hey sighed heavily.

"It's true," said Lesmes, contradicting the incredulity of his listeners. "The news programme was tracking it. It was all the country needed."

A very long silence followed his words.

Lesmes ordered another round of beer. The serving girl brought them, unhappily. Lesmes explained that he would travel with a military convoy, back to Teruel, and from there he would go on to Bogotá.

"I hope they don't blow us up on the way," he said.

And again, silence, while we drank.

I was about to take my leave, when he started up again.

"It's this country," he said, licking his sparse moustache. "If you go down the list, president by president, they've all screwed up."

Nobody answered.

Lesmes, who really felt like talking, answered himself.

"Yes," he said, "when it comes to the crunch every president fucked things up, each in his own way. Why? I don't know, who can know? Egotism, stupidity? But history will take their portraits down off the walls. Because, when it comes time for tea . . . "

"What tea, damn it," said Chepe, growing exasperated. "Coffee, at least."

"When it comes time for tea," Lesmes carried on, unperturbed, dazzled by his own words, "no-one has any faith." And he downed his beer in one gulp.

He waited for someone to say something, but we all remained silent.

"San José still is and will go on being vulnerable," he added. "The only thing I recommend to everyone is to get out, and the sooner the better. He who wants to die, stay."

He was still forgetting about the kidnapping of Chepe's wife, who had given birth in captivity.

Chepe dismissed him then and there, in his way, with a shout, and kicked the bottle-covered table.

"First, you get the hell out of my shop, you son of a bitch," he told him, and jumped on him.

I saw, in front of me, the others pulling them apart. Hey smiled to himself, expectant.

But Lesmes was right: for anyone who wanted to die, here was his tomb, where he stood.

As for me, it does not matter. I am already dead.

Saturday? The young doctor has also left San José, as have the nurses. No-one remains in charge of the improvised hospital. And the Red Cross trucks, which supplied the population with food and fuel, have not been back to visit us. We have had news of another skirmish, a few kilometres from here, near Maestro Claudino's cabin. There were twelve deaths. Twelve. And among the twelve a child. It will not be long before they come back, that we know, and who will come back? It does not matter, they will come back.

The contingents of soldiers, who while away their time in San José, for months, as if it were reborn peacetime, have been considerably reduced. In any case, with them or without them the events of war will always loom, intensified. If we see fewer soldiers, we are not informed of this in an official way; the only declaration from the authorities is that everything is under control; we hear it on the news – on small battery-operated radios, because we still have no electricity – we read it in the delayed newspapers; the President affirms that nothing is happening here, neither here nor anywhere in the country is there a war; according to him Otilia is not missing, and Mauricio Rey, Dr Orduz, Sultana and Fanny the school caretaker and so many others of this town died of old age, and I laugh again, why do I laugh just when I discover that all I want to do is sleep without waking? It is fear, this fear, this country, which I prefer to ignore in its entirety, playing the idiot with myself, to stay alive, or with an apparent desire to stay alive, because it is very possible, really, that I am dead, I tell myself, good and dead in hell, and I laugh again.

Wednesday? Two army patrols, operating separately, attacked each other, and all due to a bad informant, who warned of the presence of guerrillas on the outskirts of town: four soldiers died and several were injured. Rodrigo Pinto, our neighbour up on the mountain, came to visit me, alarmed: he told me that Captain Berrío, in his district, accompanied by soldiers, warned that if he found evidence of collaborators he was going to take steps, and he said it in person, shack by shack, interrogating not just the men and women but children under four, who barely knew how to talk.

"He's mad," Rodrigo told me.

"Truly mad. He wasn't removed from his post as we all thought he would be," I tell him. "I saw him shoot civilians with my own eyes."

"Mad, but that doesn't surprise us," says Rodrigo. "Far from town, in the mountains, what surprises us is that we're still alive."

Rodrigo Pinto, who went with me and helped to bury Maestro Claudino, a week after I found him decapitated, dead in the company of his dog, on the blue mountain, where you still see vultures circling around, swears that despite the sorrows he is not going to leave the mountain, and that his wife agrees.

"There we'll stay," he says.

We are talking at the edge of the cliff, on the outskirts of town, where Rodrigo will select the path that will take him back up to his mountain. He repeats that he is not leaving, as if he wanted to convince himself, or as if trying to get me to back up his proposal, his possibly lethal obstinacy in staying.

"Another mountain would be better," he says, "further away, even further, much further away."

He took a bottle of aguardiente out of his bag and offered me a swig. Night was falling.

"You see that mountain?" he asked, pointing to the

distant peak of another mountain, in the middle of the rest, but much further away, inland: "I'm going to go there. It's far. Good thing. I'm going up to the top of it, and nobody will fucking see me again. I have a good machete. I only need to take a pregnant sow, a cockerel and a hen, like Noah. And my wife wants to come with me, we won't be short of yucca. You see the mountain, don't you, *profesor*? Beautiful, productive mountain. That mountain could be my life. My father raised me in the mountains. For now I'll stay on the neighbouring mountain, *profesor*. You know it, you've been there, you know I live there with my wife and children; the next one's been born now, there are seven of us now, but even if it's just on yucca and cacao, we are going to survive. We'll be expecting you there, when you have your Otilia with you. Then we'll all go, why don't we all go?"

We have another drink, finish it off, and Rodrigo throws the empty bottle into the ravine. But he still does not leave: stony, his eyes on the distant mountain. He squeezes his white hat tightly in his hands, twists it: his characteristic gesture. And then he scratches his head, and his voice changes.

"Dreams don't cost anything," he says, and, almost immediately: "Wake up," and we both laugh.

It was at that moment the little soldier appeared; he was, in fact, a boy, almost a uniformed child. He had probably been beside us the whole time, without our noticing. But he seemed agitated, and he had his finger on the trigger, although he was pointing his rifle at the ground.

"What are you laughing at?" he asked us. "What's so funny? Do I look as if I'm joking?"

Rodrigo and I looked at each other slack-jawed. And laughed some more. Inevitable.

"Friend," I said to the soldier, and I suffered, in my eyes, his opaque, sharp eyes, "now you're not going to tell us we cannot laugh."

I shook Rodrigo's hand heartily, in farewell. Rodrigo put on his white hat and set off along the path, without turning round to look. He had a long walk ahead of him. I returned home, with the soldier behind me, in silence. I sensed that they were keeping an eye on Rodrigo, and, by extension, they were keeping an eye on me. Just a block from my house another group of soldiers came to meet me; were they going to arrest me, as on the day I got up too early?

"Let him go on," I heard Captain Berrío say.

Tuesday? Others are leaving now: General Palacios and his "troop" of animals. Hey tells us at Chepe's that he witnessed the evacuation of General Palacios' most valuable animals by helicopter. Ever since the arrival of this general, whom we almost never saw, we knew that he had devoted body and soul to developing a zoo; a zoo we never saw, or which we only saw in black-and-white photographs, in the pages of a Sunday newspaper. And we read that there were sixty ducks, seventy tortoises, ten caimans, twenty-seven herons, five stone-curlews, twelve capybaras, thirty dairy cattle and a hundred and ninety horses on the hundred hectares of the San José military garrison, in the care of the General and his men. Military medics attended this contingent of bipeds and quadrupeds. Every morning, in the company of his pure-bred dog imported from the United States, the General did the rounds of the garrison to supervise closely the care of his animals. A macaw was his special favourite: so spoilt that he put an officer in charge of its diet, but so inquisitive that it was electrocuted on the garrison's perimeter fence. Ever since he was a colonel, Palacios has been devoted to animals.

He also claims to have planted more than five thousand trees.

"As if he planted them himself," Hey says, and also tells us that he saw Hortensia Galindo and her twins leave town in one of those cargo helicopters, full of animals.

"Good morning, *profesor*. I've come to say goodbye."

At the door is Gloria Dorado, a cloth hat in her hands, her eyes red from crying. She carries a wooden cage, with a troupial inside.

"I want to give you this as a memento, *profesor*, so you can take care of him."

I take the cage. It is the first time I have received a cage as a memento: as soon as we are alone I shall let you go, bird, how am I going to take care of you? I can barely take care of myself.

"Come in, Gloria. We'll have a cup of coffee."

"I don't have time, *profesor*."

"And your house? What is going to happen to your house?"

"I have entrusted it to Lucrecia, in case I come back. Although it could be that she will leave too, of course.

But she can use the house, she has five children, and I have none, *profesor*. And I probably won't have any."

"You never know, Gloria. You are young and beautiful. You've got your whole life ahead of you."

She smiles sadly.

"You've still got your sense of humour, *profesor*. I'm very fond of you both, and I know that Otilia will be back, I swear."

"Everybody tells me so."

I cannot keep the grief out of my voice; I wished Gloria had not come to say it again. She does not realize.

"I dreamt I saw you walking together, in the market. I felt happy and went to say hello. I said to you: 'Didn't I tell you Otilia would return safe and sound?'"

She smiles, she smiles at me, and I must confess her dream hurts me, are we going to cry? That's all I need.

"God willing," I say, the cage hanging from my hand: the troupial hops from one side to the other, sits on the tiny bamboo swing, and begins to sing: perhaps he has guessed my intention to set him free. "And how are you going, Gloria?" I ask, and can no longer look her in the eye. "There is no circulation allowed on the highway. They threaten to blow up any vehicle, private or not, and sometimes with the occupants inside. There is no secure transport."

"A lieutenant has offered to take us, my sister and

me, as far as El Palo, in his truck, with the soldiers. I'll find transport from there to go inland."

"Travelling in a truck like that will be just as dangerous, if not more so. You'll be exposed, Gloria. Do not even think of disguising yourself as a soldier: how can this lieutenant take you that way, putting you at risk?"

"He told me in secret that the truck will be protected by warplanes. They'll clear the way for us, *profesor*."

"I hope so."

"And I will be in more danger here," Gloria says; her eyes mist up and she whispers: "when they find out that Marcos turned up dead. Hortensia will not forgive me, she'll say that I'm guilty, she'll say I killed him."

Now she begins to cry, hugs me, and I hug her, wrapping my arms around her with the cage in one hand

"He showed up in a ditch, half a kilometre from here. It took a while to recognize him. According to what the Lieutenant told me, he's been dead for two years, at least, left out there, in that ditch."

"Gloria. Another death, by force. To the shame of the living."

"You see, *profesor*? They didn't want to help him. No-one moved a finger to get him freed. That woman didn't offer a single peso for her husband. I didn't have money, just that little house he gave me. But what good is all that money to her? It won't be long before they take her too."

I do not want to tell her that Hortensia Galindo has already left San José, and in a helicopter.

"Oh, Gloria, this country, poor in its wealth. Good luck, start your life over again. What else can I say?"

"Like telling someone to be born again," she smiles. "Is that what you're advising?" And she pulls away.

I am pervaded by her fertile, torrid perfume, mixed with the smell of her tears.

"I'm off," she says, "my sister is waiting." And she leaves the house.

I close the door.

I go, cage in hand, to the garden. I am seized by a sort of annoyance: let beautiful women not come to this house, let my pain not be increased by seeing them, damn it. I put the cage down on the stone laundry sink, and open the tiny bamboo door.

"Fly away, troupial," I shout at the bird. "Hurry up and fly, or the Survivors will come and take care of you."

The bird stays still, before the open door.

"Aren't you going to fly? You'll see, there are cats here."

The bird remains motionless. Have his wings been cut? I cover him with my hand and take him out of the cage. It is a lovely troupial, his feathers gleam, his wings are not cut.

"Are you frightened of the sky? fly, for God's sake," and I throw him up into the sky.

The troupial, taken by surprise, spreads his still numb wings, and, with great effort, manages to cushion the fall. Then he hops, a couple of times, and at last flies, as if jumping, up to the wall. There again he stays still: what is he waiting for? It is as if he was turning back to look at me, at the cage.

"What a lovely bird," says a voice.

It is Geraldina, appearing through the breach in the wall, Geraldina dressed in black. I no longer remember her naked.

"A troupial," I say.

And we both see him fly, disappear into the sky.

Once again sitting in the middle of the rubble, beside each other; her face at my side encloses me, without our taking our eyes off the sky. "Those were other times," I tell her, and I can believe she knows what I'm referring to: her walking naked in her garden, me peering over the wall.

She gives a faint laugh and then the same pensive face reappears, her eyes on the sky as it fills with clouds, eyes on the skyless clouds; I see a hand on her knee, it is my hand on her knee, when did I put my hand on her knee? But she does not respond, it is the same as if a withered leaf had fallen from a tree and landed on her leg, a disgusting but innocuous insect, and she keeps talking (since when?) of her negotiations with those who are holding her husband prisoner, or an old man's hand landing on her knee all of a sudden seems quite natural to her, old age has its liberties, or simply the only thing that interests her in this world is the payment of the ransom, the enterprise in which she is now involved, with the support of her brother from Buga; that is why, Ismael, no wonder she does not see my hand on her knee, she assures me she has given them all she has, she says she is at a crossroads, don't you worry, *profesor*, it is my crossroads. Then she stares at me attentively, as if she guessed or thought she had guessed my thoughts; has she perhaps discovered my hand on her knee? Does she now know that I am only thinking of her knee? The contact, the flame?

"No, *profesor*," she tells me. "They do not have Otilia. I asked them."

"Otilia," I say.

Now she tells me that she was not even able to raise half the money they were demanding.

"Don't bother even giving us half," they told her. "You won't be doing your husband any favours," they said, she tells me, her mouth contracted into a rictus I have never seen before; is it joy? They even said to her: "It's obvious you don't love him."

She tells me: "I felt their looks all over my body, *profesor*, as if they wanted to eat me alive."

They gave her two weeks to pay the rest, "that means today, *profesor*, time's up today, I told them I agreed, and I told them to bring him with them, as they promised before, a promise they broke."

"And what if we had brought him?" they answered. "We would have had to take him back again. If we didn't feel like it, his death would be your fault, for failing to comply, understand?"

I told them again to bring him, to let me see him, speak to him, and I said: "I already gave you all I had, now I have to find someone to lend me more, and if no-one will lend me money, I'll still be here with my son."

"What do you mean, they won't lend it to you?" they said. "You'll see."

Geraldina looks at me again with a shocked, terrified expression; I do not know what to say to her; I have never seen the faces of the kidnappers; who knows what kind of people they are?

I only met Geraldina's brother; I saw him arrive from Buga in his car, a rainy night; tall, bald, worried;

he managed to cross the last stretch of highway with a safe-conduct pass from the guerrillas; I heard him sound his horn three times and looked out of the window: Geraldina came out, with a candle in her hand; they embraced. And they went into the house, both carrying, with effort, an enormous black plastic bag, with Geraldina's money in cash, her money and her husband's, she told me with sudden fury, the money earned by the couple through years of work, *profesor*, never any wrongdoing.

The same night of his arrival, Geraldina's brother, a startled shadow, left San José the same way he came, in his car, in the rain, the safe-conduct taped to the inside of the windscreen as if it were a flag. He argued with Geraldina about the advisability of leaving Eusebito with her. Geraldina was willing to let him go, but the boy wanted to stay with his mother.

"I explained to him what the risks were, I explained it to him as to a little man." Geraldina is proud, in her innocence. "And Eusebito had no hesitations: with his papa and his mama till death." Geraldina's mouth half opens, her eyes go further off into the sky: "I haven't got a peso left, *profesor*, that's what I'm going to tell them, they'll have to take pity, and if they don't take pity, let them do what they want, let them take me with him, that would be preferable, the three of us together, as it was meant to be, than to wait years not knowing how long, and Eusebito will go with me, that's my last card, they'll take pity, I'm sure, I've given them everything, I'm not hiding anything from them."

Now Geraldina has begun to cry: for the second time today a woman is crying in this house.

And while she cries I see my hand on her knee, without really seeing it – I discover that, in one second – but all of a sudden I see it, my hand still on Geraldina's knee. Geraldina, who cries and does not see or does not want to see my hand on her knee, or she is seeing it now, Ismael, you are so shabby that all that matters is her knee, never the tears for her missing husband, not even Geraldina's senseless but irrefutable joy: to say that her son will accompany her like a little man, whatever may happen, and to say it without her voice breaking, what would her husband think? What a disappointment: "Pack up everything and get out of here," something like that Eusebito said his father said, Geraldina's delirious voice moves me, the two of us in the middle of the ruins, among the remains of flowers, both the same.

"Hortensia offered me a lift in the helicopter with her, *profesor*. Of course, I am not taking it, I could not. But today I won't deny it: I am afraid."

She is staring at my hand on her knee.

"You," she says, or asks.

"Yes?"

And again the fleeting laugh.

"You're not going to die, *profesor?*"

"No."

"Look how you're trembling."

"It is the emotion, Geraldina. Or it is my lechery, as Otilia would say."

"Don't worry, *profesor*. Stick with love. Love conquers lechery."

And, tenderly, I remove my hand from her knee. But she stays there, in silence, sitting beside me.

Her son called her, from the other side of the wall: it seemed he had just fallen in the empty pool, or was it a game? His voice sounded as if he had just fallen into the pool, and then a shout, nothing more. Geraldina returned immediately, ducking through the breach in the wall, her body as if carved in mourning. I did not follow her: another would have, not me, not any more: what for? Besides, I was hungry, hungry for the first time; when was the last time I ate? I went to the kitchen and looked for the pot of rice: there was one plateful left, the grains looked hard, damp, burnt. I ate them with my hand, cold, leathery, and I sat there for a while, in front of the stove. For a long time now the

Survivors had not appeared in the house, no doubt due to the lack of food, of attention. They would have to take care of themselves. But I missed their meowing and their eyes, which brought me close to Otilia, kept me company: thinking of them was like invoking their memory, palpable in the kitchen, where traces of feathers, like a trail in a fairy tale, led me into my bedroom: there, at the foot of the bed, lay two mangled birds, and on the pillow, the remains of black butterflies, an offering of food the cats had left for me. This is all I needed, I thought, for my cats to feed me: if I do not take care of their lunch, they take care of mine. If I had not eaten that rice, I would not have hesitated to finish plucking those birds and roast them. I picked up the birds, the butterflies, swept up the feathers, then I wanted to sleep, I stretched out face down, I think I was just about asleep when a woman's scream from the street summoned me, everyone is screaming, I said to myself, and left the house as if stepping out into hell.

A woman was running, pressing her apron against her thighs – or wiping her hands on her apron – what was she fleeing? She was not fleeing, but running, because she wanted to see something.

"Have you heard, *profesor?*" she said.

I followed her. I wanted to see too. We arrived at Chepe's shop, and there, sitting in the aisle, before the tables, which were in disorder as if they had been blown about by a gale, Chepe clutched his head in his hand, surrounded by onlookers. "They must have found his wife, but dead," I thought, as I saw him in the midst of desperation: it was not hot; an abnormal wind responded to Chepe's hoarse groaning, and the dust swirled around his shoes. The small group of men and women were waiting: it was like a lacerated silence, because the questions would return, the timid comments. I too had questions: early that morning they had delivered to Chepe, under the door, like a final warning, the index fingers of his wife and daughter in a bloody paper bag. I want to give Chepe my condolences, but Hey approaches from among those present and takes me by the arm. The last thing I want is to chat with Hey, especially in these circumstances, but his dazed face, his hands on me, convince me; I remembered how I had felt sorry for him the last time I spoke to him, in a similar way, without remembering who he was, or why.

"*Profesor*," he said into my ear, "they didn't kill you while you slept?"

"Of course not," I managed to say once I had recovered from the question. And I tried to laugh: "Do you not see that I am here with you?"

And, nevertheless, we stood looking at each other for a few seconds, as if we could not believe it.

"And who was going to kill me?" I asked. "And why?"

"That's what I was told," he replied.

He did not seem drunk, or drugged. Pale, his good eye blinked, without taking it off mine. His hands would not let go of my arm.

"What kind of joke is this?" I asked.

And he: "Then you're alive, *profesor*."

"Still," I said.

And he, out of the blue: "You know something? I've never killed anyone."

"What?" I asked.

He said: "Pure lies, to attract customers."

I remembered with difficulty what he was referring to. "Well, you drove them away," I said. "We all thought you sliced throats."

I pulled my arm out of his hands. No-one was listening to us.

"I'm glad you're alive, *profesor*," he went on to say.

He looked like a punished child, provoking inexplicable pity. I left him there, with his unprecedented question, his blinking eye; he turned his back on the people and left; I forgot him.

"So they killed me while I slept," I said aloud, and for an instant I was convinced I was telling Otilia: "I never had that pleasure."

Chepe clutches the bag and stands up, his lips stretched as if he were laughing in astonishment. And he walks rapidly, followed by men and women. Where? I follow him too, like the rest. He has to go somewhere.

"He's going to the police station," someone surmises.

"What for?" says someone else.

"To ask them."

"Ask them what? They're not going to answer."

"What can they answer?"

In the middle of this circle of bodies, of faces that understand nothing, and which are prepared to understand nothing, near the police-station door, I see myself, another body, another dazed face. As if by common accord we have allowed Chepe to go in alone. He goes in, and comes out again almost at once, his face contorted. We realize before he says anything: there is not a single policeman in the post, where did they go? It did seem strange that there was not an agent or two at the entrance: for the first time we perceive that this silence is too much in San José, a cloud of alarm runs through us all, equally, in all the faces, in the faded voices. I remember Gloria Dorado was leaving in a military truck; was it perhaps the last truck? They did not say anything to us, no warning, and everyone else seems to be thinking the same thing I am: at whose mercy have we been left?

We only now discover that the streets are being invaded by slow silent figures, which emerge blurry from the last horizon of the corners, appear here, there, almost lazy, vanish for a time and reappear, numerous, from the edges of the cliff. Then those of us surrounding Chepe begin our retreat, also slowly and silently, each to his own, to their houses, and, what is extraordinary, we do so as if it is the most natural thing in the world.

"Everybody to the plaza," one of the henchmen yells, but it is as if nobody were listening.

I walk behind a couple, without recognizing them, and I remain beside them, not bothering to find out in which direction they are walking.

"I said everybody to the plaza," the voice calls again, from a different place.

Nobody pays any attention; we hear our own increasingly keen footsteps: from one moment to the next people are running, and I among them, this old man that I am.

"After all, we are unarmed," I say. "What can we do?" I have said it aloud and enraged, as if excusing myself to Otilia.

We who were with Chepe no longer see him, but then we hear him: at the top of his voice, screaming, squealing like a hog near slaughter, hair-raising because it comes from a terrified man, he is asking the invaders if they are the ones who have his wife and daughter, if they are the ones who sent him the fingers of his wife and daughter that morning, he asks them and we stop, a majority, like a truce, on different corners, no-one can believe it, the wind keeps propelling shreds of dust along the pavements, the sun hides behind a band of clouds. It might rain, I think. Send down a flood, Lord, and drown us all.

We do not see Chepe, or I do not see him. The motionless bodies of men and women, the bodies of the invaders, block him from view, but we do hear his voice, which repeats the question, this time followed by curses and accusations, from Chepe, to our sorrow, to his sorrow, because we hear a shot.

"There goes Chepe," says the man beside me.

The woman is already running, and then the man, and again everyone, in different directions, but no-one screams, no-one cries out, all in silence, as if trying not to make any noise as they run.

"To the plaza, damn it," says another voice.

The men in uniform are also running, herding the people, as if we were cattle, nobody can believe it, but it has to be believed, it does: the couple beside me find their house at last, on the other side of the church.

I want to go in with them; the man stops me.

"Not you, *profesor*," he says. "You go to your own house, or you'll get us into trouble."

What is he saying, I wonder, and I see his enormous head in profile, his frightened eyes, and his wife's hands appear and help him and they close the door in my face. The man does not want to allow me to enter his house, this is his fear, I am someone who can get them into trouble, he said. I am alone again, it would appear: do not lose, Ismael, the memory of the streets that lead back home. In vain I look at all the corners: it is all the same corner, the same danger, they look identical. Misfortune might emerge from any one of them again. I head down one of the streets: do not go the wrong way, Ismael; I return as if feeling my way back to my own house, during a long night, it is extraordinary, the street is empty; only me, along the edge of doors and windows shut tight. I knock on the closed shutters of one of those windows: does not old Celmiro, older than me, a friend, live here? Yes, I find, to my relief, it is a miracle, Celmiro's house, Celmiro will let me come in. And I bang against the broad wooden frame: a sliver hurts my fist, but no-one opens the window, I know it is the window of Celmiro's room.

I hear someone clearing his throat, and put my ear to the crack.

"Celmiro," I say. "Is that you? Open the window."

No-one answers.

"There isn't time to go to the door," I say. "I'm coming in the window."

"Ismael? Did they not kill you while you slept?"

"Of course not, who made that up?"

"That's what I heard."

"Open up, Celmiro. Hurry."

"And how do you think I'm going to do that, Ismael? I'm dying."

I am still alone in the middle of the street. And what is worse, I do not have the strength to keep fleeing. The noise is getting louder, I think, approaching from somewhere, it will not be long before it envelops me.

"What is happening out there, Ismael? I heard shots and shrieks: are they dancing in the streets?"

"They are killing, Celmiro."

"And you, did they make you dance too?"

"I should think so."

"The best thing would be to go home, I can't move. Half my body is paralysed, didn't you know?"

"No."

"You didn't hear what my disgraceful children did either? They left me here. They brought over a pot of rice and fried plantain, a pan of liver and kidneys, and then they left me lying here. They did leave me a lot of meat, so I could eat, but what do I do when it runs out? The wretches."

"At least open the window. I'll come in through the window. We'll protect ourselves."

"Protect ourselves from whom?"

"I told you, they're killing people."

"They were right to leave."

"Open the window, Celmiro."

"Didn't I tell you I can't move? Thrombosis, Ismael, do you know what that is? I am older than you. Look at you, after all: out in the street, and dancing."

"Open up."

"I can only move my right arm, to take a piece of meat, what will I do when I need to relieve myself?"

"Here they come, shooting in all directions."

"Wait."

Time goes by. I hear something fall, inside.

"Damn," I hear Celmiro say.

"What happened?"

"The frying pan with the kidneys fell. If a dog gets in here I won't be able to frighten it away. It'll eat everything."

He is weeping or swearing.

"What about the window, Celmiro?"

"I can't reach."

"Open it, you can."

"Run, Ismael, run somewhere, for God's sake, if what you're saying is true, but don't stand there wasting time. A dog will get in, sooner or later, and eat everything, will I have to wet the bed?"

"Goodbye, Celmiro."

But I stay still. I do not hear the noise any more.

I will try to drag myself, at least. I do not have the strength to run, as Celmiro advises.

"Your children will come back," I tell him, in farewell.

"That's what they said, but why did they leave all this food beside me, what did they leave it for? They left San José, they left me. They are wretches."

I lean against the front of each house, in order to go on. I discover it all of a sudden, it is the noise, congealed; I am not alone in the street: the compact voices return, I turn round, they are voices that twist and tangle neither very nearby nor too far away, a river all over, and I catch sight of them, two blocks away: I see them go past, a small tumult of purplish faces and open mouths, in profile; I do not see who is screaming, they pass like a maelstrom in the middle of the fleeting noise, for now nothing can be heard, just the most private noises, an almost inaudible sigh; now the pursuers appear, and the last of them have turned in my direction, they are running, they advance on me, have they found me? They search, hunt, just half a block away, they point their weapons in every direction, they want to fire, they are going to shoot into the air, or are they going to shoot me? They point everywhere with their guns, they want to fire, I slump to the pavement and stay there curled up in a ball as if I were asleep, pretending to be dead, I pretend to be dead, I am dead, I am not asleep, it really is as though my own heart were not beating, I do not even close my eyes: I leave them wide open, motionless, immersed in the sky with its swirling clouds, and I hear the sound of boots, nearby, the same as fear, as if the air around me had disappeared; one of them must be looking at me, examining me now from the tip of my shoes to the last hair on my head, he will use my bones for target practice, I think, on the verge of making myself laugh, free again and simply, like a sneeze, in vain I press my lips together, I feel I am about to laugh louder than I ever have in my life, the men walk past as if they do not see me, or think I am dead, I do not know how I can contain the burst of laughter, the laughter of fear, and only after a minute of playing dead, or two, I turn my head to one side, move my gaze: the group runs off round the corner, I listen to the first drops of rain, fat, isolated, falling like big wrinkled flowers that explode in the dust: the flood, Lord, the deluge, but the drops stop at once and I tell myself *God does not agree*, and again on the verge of laughter, on the verge, it is your madness, Ismael, I say, and the laughter inside me stops, as if I were ashamed of myself.

"We don't have to bother killing this old man, don't you see? He looks dead."

"Shall we give him a good whack?"

"Isn't that the same old man we saw dead a minute ago? Yeah, it's the same one. Look how pink he is, he doesn't smell dead, maybe he's a saint."

"Hey, old man, are you alive, or are you dead?"

I was not alone. They were there, behind me. The man who said that put the barrel of his gun against my neck. I heard him laugh, but I kept still.

"What if we tickle him?"

"No, you don't tickle saints. We'll come back later, old man, and we won't be in such a good mood."

"Better just whack him and get it over with."

"If you're going to kill me, kill me."

"Hear that? The dead man spoke."

"Didn't I tell you? A saint, a miracle from God. Is he hungry? Wouldn't you like a little bit of bread? Ask God."

They are leaving. I think they are leaving.

God, bread?

Worm food.

No. They are not leaving.

I am startled, without looking at them directly. I hear them return, taking an age, to my side. They have settled on something abominable among them. They drag over a body and drop it down beside me. He must be very badly wounded: his face and chest bathed in blood. It is someone from the town, someone I know, but who?

"Well," says one of the men to me.

Well?

And the man: "Do him the favour of killing him."

He hands me a pistol, which I do not take:

"I've never killed anyone."

"Kill me, papá," shouts the wounded man, with great effort, as if he is already speaking to me from much further away, and he rolls on to his side, trying in vain to look me in the eye; the tears prevent him from doing so, the blood that covers his face.

"You kill him," I say to the one offering me the pistol. "Can you not see that he is suffering? Finish what you started."

I sit up as best I can. I have never felt my own weight as such a burden; my arms crumple, my legs; but I still have the strength to push away the pistol they offer me, strength to spurn the gun, which has been pointing at me all the while.

I start to move away, again feeling my way; I flee with exasperating slowness, because my body is not my own; where am I fleeing to? Up, down?

And I hear the shot. The bullet whistles past just above my head; and then another, which hits the ground, centimetres from my shoe. I stop, and turn round to look. I am amazed that I do not feel afraid.

"That's what I'm starting to like about you, old man: you don't tremble. But now I know why. You're not capable of shooting yourself, are you? You want us to kill you, to do you that favour. And we're not going to give you that pleasure, now, are we?"

The others say no, laughing. I hear the wounded man groan, as if neighing weakly. I start away again, staggering.

Another shot.

This time it was not aimed at me.

I turn round to look.

"Who is this old son of a bitch?" they keep saying.

"Hey, old man, do you want us to do some target practice on you?"

"Here," I tell them and point to my heart.

I do not know what they find funny this time: my face? They reply with another guffaw.

Where am I? Not only do I hear once more the confused clamour, which rises and falls now and again, and the shots, indistinct, but also the calls of Hey, who has lost his mind – I assume, even as I am going to lose mine, like everyone — but how can he be trying to sell his empanadas in the midst of this chaos, I wonder, when I hear the *Heeeey* that settles in all the streets, incredibly clear, as if Hey himself were on every corner: I cannot recognize the town, it is another town now, similar, but other, brimming with artifice, astonishment, a town with neither head nor heart, which corner of this town to choose? It would be best to follow a single direction until I was out of it, will I be able? Now I discover it is not only fatigue, lack of determination that keeps me from going on. It is my knee, again. There is no cure for old age, Maestro Claudino, may you rest in peace.

By the school I find a group of people walking in single file, in the direction of the highway. They are leaving San José: they must be thinking the same way I am; it is a large portion of the population that is leaving. Slow and depleted — men, women, old folks, children — they no longer run. They are a shadow of bewildered faces in suspense, before me; the ladies stammer out prayers, one or two men insist on carrying the most valuable belongings, clothes, provisions, even a television set. Aren't you leaving, *profesor*? No, I am staying, I hear myself decide. And here I stay between the hot shade of the abandoned houses, the mute trees, I say goodbye to all of them waving this hand, I am staying, God, I am staying, I stay because only here can I find you, Otilia, only here can I wait for you, and if you do not come, you do not come, but I am staying here.

"Be careful, *profesor*," the same man who closed his door in my face when we were running away tells me.

It is not the first time they come to offer me that advice.

The man insists.

"They have a list of names. Every one they find has had it, just like that."

"*Profesor*," another decides. "You're on the list. They're searching for you. Better come with us, and keep quiet."

It is a surprise. They are searching for me. I look at the one who has spoken: one of Celmiro's sons.

"What about your father?" I ask him. "You left him?"

"He didn't want to come, *profesor*. We wanted to carry him, but he said he would rather die where he was born, rather than die somewhere else."

And he looks me in the eye, without blinking. His voice falters.

"If he told you that his children were wretches, it's not true; he likes to complain. Go and see, *profesor*. The house is open. He wouldn't let us carry him."

Who to believe?

Including Celmiro's son, there are just three inhabitants of this town who are still standing by me. But they begin to rush me, irritated.

"Come with us, *profesor*. Don't be stubborn."

"How?" I say, and show them my swollen knee. "Even if I wanted to I could not."

Celmiro's son shrugs and jogs away after the group. The other two sigh, shake their heads.

"They'll soon turn up, *profesor*. Don't you tell them who you are. No-one's going to recognize you."

"What about Chepe?" I say. "What happened in the end? I did not see what happened to him."

"We never saw him."

"Who is going to bury the dead? Who buried Chepe?"

"None of us buried him."

And I hear one of them say, ironically: "It must have been one of them."

"The one who killed him, most likely."

They regret saying it, or feel sorry for me, from the expression I must have on my face, while listening to them.

"We're going, *profesor*, we don't want to die. What can we do? They ordered us to leave, and we have to leave, as simple as that."

"Come with us, *profesor*. You're on the list. We heard

your name. Be careful. Your name was there."

Why do they ask for names? They kill whoever they please, no matter what their names might be. I would like to know what is written on the paper with the names, that "list". It is a blank sheet of paper, for God's sake. A paper where all the names they want can fit.

A sound of voices and breathing wells up from one side of the school, from the dense bank that adjoins the trees, the mountains, the immensity, wells up from the narrow path that comes down from the mountain range: more sweating men and women are arriving to join the line, I hear their voices, they talk and tremble, complain, lament,

"They're killing people like flies," they say, as if we did not know.

In vain I look for Rodrigo Pinto and his wife and their children. In vain I search for Rodrigo and his dream, his mountain. I ask after him: one of his neighbours shakes his head, and does not do so sadly, as I would have expected. On the contrary, he seems about to tell a joke: he tells me he saw his hat floating in the river, and keeps walking along with the rest, ignoring further questions. "And Rodrigo's wife, his children?" I insist, limping after them.

"There were seven," he yells, without turning around.

*

I see them disappear around the first bend in the road. They are leaving, I am staying, is there really any difference? They will go somewhere, to a place that is not theirs, that will never be theirs, like what is happening to me, staying in a place which is no longer mine: here dusk or night might begin to fall or dawn to break without my knowing, is it that I no longer remember the time? My days in San José, when I am the only one in its streets, will be hopeless.

If I could at least come across Celmiro's window again, we could keep each other company, but where? I no longer know. I examine the corners, the façades: I catch sight of the Survivors, coming round the gutter on the roof of a house, one beside the other, above me, keeping pace with me, and observing me in turn, their eyes filled with curiosity, as if they recognized me too.

"Oh, to be a cat, God, just a cat up there on the roof," I say to them. "They'll surely shoot at me before they shoot at you two."

They listen to me and disappear, as swiftly as they appeared, were they following me?

From the trees a cluster of birds takes flight, after a series of bursts of gunfire, still distant. Far away, another group of stragglers, men and women, rush along the road: it looks as if they are fleeing on tiptoe, trying not to make any noise, with voluntary, disproportionate stealth. Some of the women point to me, terrified, as if commenting to each other on the presence of a ghost. I have sat down on a flat, white rock, under a fragrant magnolia tree; I do not remember this rock either, or this magnolia, when did they appear? With every reason I do not know this street, these corners, things, I have lost my memory, just as if I were sinking and I began to walk one by one down steps which lead to the most unknown, this town, I shall stay alone, I suppose, but in some way I shall make this town my home, and I shall stroll through you, town, until Otilia comes for me.

I shall eat what they have left in their kitchens, I shall sleep in all their beds, I shall recognize their stories by their vestiges, guessing at their lives from the clothes they left behind, my time shall be another time, I shall amuse myself, I am not blind, I shall cure my knee, I shall walk up to the high plateau as a stroll and then return, my cats will continue to feed me, if weeping is all that is left, let it be out of happiness; am I going to cry? No, just burst out laughing with all the unpredictable laughter I have been holding back all this time, and I am going to laugh because I have just seen my daughter, beside me, you have sat down on this rock, I tell her, I hope you understand all the horror that I am, inside, "or all the love" – this last I say out loud, laughing – I hope you are drawing near in sympathy with me, that you forgive the only one guilty of the disappearance of your mother, because I left her on her own.

Now I see Otilia in front of me.

And with her some children who must be my grandchildren and who look at me appalled, all holding hands.

"Are you real?" I ask them. This is all I could ask them.

Hey's shout replies, fleeting, unexpected. The vision of Otilia vanishes, leaving a bitter trace on my tongue, as if I had just swallowed something truly bitter, the laughter, my laughter.

I stand up. I shall walk to my house. If this town has gone, my house has not. I am going there, I say, I shall go, though I may be lost.

Two or three streets away from the white rock, from which I should perhaps never have moved, I meet the same men who know I am not dead, I meet them in the middle of the street, before a house with geraniums growing by the door, whose house? List in hand they call someone at the tops of their voices, a name I do not recognize, mine? I carry on walking towards them, and realize my stupidity too late, when it would be more than reckless to turn back; but they do not give me a second glance; I see from where I am that the door to the house is open. With a last effort I make for the opposite pavement, against the wall, under the shadows of a row of overturned tables: Chepe's place, again.

They keep shouting the name, the door remains open, nobody comes out, nobody obeys the name, the fatal order. One of the armed men walks over and unnecessarily kicks in the door, smashes it with the butt of his rifle; he goes inside followed by two or three others. They drag out a man I do not recognize, they repeat his name, who? Am I forgetting even the names? It is a young man with a moustache, more frightened than I am, pale, they leave him sitting in the street, the wind moves his shirt tails strangely – separate animals, waving goodbye – they yell something at him that I do not understand because behind it comes a woman's scream bursting out of the house, an old woman comes out, Otilia's age, I must know who she is, his mother? Yes, his mother comes out after him, berating the henchmen.

"But he has done nothing," she screams.

In any case, without hesitation, they aim at the man and fire, once, twice, three times, and then carry on walking, ignoring the mother, ignoring me; do they not want to see me? They stride away, with the mother behind them, arms flailing, her voice unhinged.

"There's still God to kill yet," she screeches at them.

"Tell us where he's hiding, little lady," they reply. She opens her mouth, when she hears them, as if gasping; then I see her doubt: should she kneel down by the body of her son, in case he is still alive, in case it is possible to comfort him in his last moment, or follow behind the men: her hand hangs from the rucksack of the last of them; with the other she points to her son's body.

"Kill him again," she screams and keeps screaming. "Why don't you kill him again?"

I have sat down on the kerb, and not because I want to play dead. The wind lifts swirls of dust again, the rain falls, softly. Somehow I stand up; I walk in the opposite direction from the mother, who screams the same thing, *Kill him again.* I hear another shot, the body falling. As when I came down from Maestro Claudino's cabin, disgust and dizziness bend me over the ground; am I in front of my own house? It is my house, I think – or, at least, the place where I sleep, that is what I want to believe. I have just gone in, only to discover that it is not my house; all the rooms have been sealed. I go back outside. Another group of men jog past, not noticing me. I stand still, listening to them run.

At last I recognize a street, near what was once a guitar factory: I find Mauricio Rey's house open, with no-one inside, all of a sudden I am convinced I am alone in town. Celmiro will have died by now: you could feel it in the air, that is what I thought: they had all gone, those who were still alive and the murderers, not a soul – I caught myself thinking, and as soon as I thought it I heard from somewhere or from everywhere Hey's cry. "He's still here," I said to myself, and the hope of finding someone reappeared.

I looked for the corner where Hey stood eternally selling his empanadas. I heard the cry, and felt again the shiver because it seemed again that it came from all places, all things, even from inside me.

"Then it is possible that I am imagining the shout," I said aloud, and heard my own voice as if it were someone else's; it is your madness, Ismael, I said, and the wind followed the cry, a cold wind, different, and Hey's corner appeared without my looking for it, on my way.

I did not see him: just the portable stove, in front of me, but the cry came again, Then I did not imagine the cry, I thought. The one who is shouting must be somewhere. Another cry, louder yet, was heard, within the corner, and multiplied with growing strength, an echo of a voice, sharp, forcing me to cover my ears. I saw the portable stove was quickly being covered by a film of red sand, a myriad of ants that zigzagged here and there, and, in the large copper frying pan, as if already before seeing it I had a premonition of it, half submerged in the cold black oil, as if petrified, Hey's head: in the middle of his forehead a shiny cockroach appeared, as the cry appeared again: this must be madness, I thought, fleeing, knowing that the cry could not really be heard, but hearing it inside, real,

real; I fled from the cry, physical, palpable, and kept hearing it lying at last in my house, on my bed, on my back, pillow over my face, covering my nose and my ears as if trying to smother myself to hear no more.

An unexpected quiet arrived, without peace: the silence all around.

It was not possible to guess what time it was, the darkness was growing, I closed my eyes: let them find me asleep, did they not kill me while I slept? But I could not get to sleep, I could not, though the earth might swallow me up. I would have to go out into the garden, look at the sky, imagine what time it might be, embrace the night, the course of things, the kitchen, the Survivors, the calm chair, to sleep again.

I went to the garden. There was still light in the sky: the saviour night was still distant.

"Geraldina," I said aloud.

Now I supposed that on the other side of the wall I should find Geraldina, and, what was absurd, find her alive, in that I trusted: to locate Geraldina, and locate her, most of all, alive. To hear her live, in spite of the screams.

But I remembered another shout: her son had called her, the last time I saw her. I remembered that as I went through the wall; the grass had grown up around it.

There was the pool; I looked into it as into a pit: amid the dead leaves that the wind blew in there, amid the bird droppings, the scattered rubbish, near the petrified corpses of the macaws, incredibly pale, face down, lay Eusebito's corpse and he was paler still because naked, his arms under his head, the blood like a thread seemed to still flow from his ear; a hen pecked about, the last hen, and she inexorably approached his face. My thoughts turned to Geraldina, and I headed for the wide-open glass door. A noise inside the house stopped me. I waited a few seconds and went on, up against the wall. Through the living room window I caught a glimpse of the profile of several men, all standing still, contemplating something with exaggerated attention, more than absorbed: gathered like parishioners in church at the hour of the Elevation. Behind them, behind their stone stillness, their shadows darkened the wall; what were they watching? Forgetting myself entirely, searching only for Geraldina, I found myself advancing towards them. Nobody took any notice of my presence; I stopped, like them, another stone sphinx, dark, emerging from the doorway. Between the arms of a wicker rocking chair, was – fully open, exhausted – Geraldina naked, her head lolling from side to side, and on top of her one of the men embracing her, one of the men delving into Geraldina, one of the men was raping her: it still took me a while to realize it was Geraldina's corpse, it was her corpse, exposed before these men who waited. Why do you not join them, Ismael? I listen to myself demean myself: why do you not explain to them how to rape a corpse? Or how to love? Is that not what you dreamt of? And I see myself lying in wait for Geraldina's naked corpse, the nakedness of the corpse that still glows, imitating perfectly what could be Geraldina's passionate embrace. These men, I thought, of whom I only saw the profiles of their deranged faces, these men must be waiting their turn, Ismael, are you too waiting for a turn? I have just asked myself that, before the corpse, while hearing her sound of a manipulated, inanimate doll – Geraldina possessed again, while the man is only a ferocious gesture, half-naked, why do you not go and tell him, not like that, why do you not go yourself and tell him how?

"O.K.," one of the men shouts, lengthening his voice strangely. "Leave it."

And another:

"Let's go."

The three or four left do not respond, they are each an island, a drooling profile: I wonder if it is not my own profile, worse than looking in the mirror.

"Goodbye, Geraldina," I say out loud, and leave.

I hear shouting at my back.

I have left by the front door. I walk towards my house, calmly walk along the street, not fleeing, not turning round to look, as if none of this were happening — while it happens — and I reach the doorknob of my house, my hands do not shake, the men shout at me not to go in.

"Freeze," they shout, surrounding me.

I feel for a second that they even fear me, and they fear me now, just when I am more alone than ever.

"Your name," they shout, "or you're finished."

Let it be finished, I only wanted, what did I want? To go inside and sleep.

Your name, they repeat.

What am I going to tell them? My name? Another name? I shall tell them I am Jesus Christ, I shall tell them I am Simón Bolívar, I shall tell them I am called Nobody, I shall tell them I have no name and I shall laugh again; they will think I am mocking them and they will shoot: this is how it will be.

ACKNOWLEDGEMENTS

The translator would like to thank Héctor Abad
Faciolince, Juan Cerezo, Juan Gabriel Vásquez
and Ben Ward for their help and advice.